I0749287

SMALL MEANS
AND
GREAT ENDS.

EDITED BY

MRS. M.H. ADAMS

Small Means and Great Ends

Edited by Mrs. M.H. Adams

PO Box 2211
Fairfield, IA 52556
www.1stworldlibrary.org
First Edition

LCCN: 2004195343

Softcover ISBN: 1-4218-0177-9
Hardcover ISBN: 1-4218-0077-2
eBook ISBN: 1-4218-0277-5

Small Means and Great Ends

contributed by Tim, Ed & Rodney

in support of

1st World Library Literary Society

Word of Truth, and Gift of Love,
Waiting hearts now need thee;
Faithful in thy mission prove,
On that mission speed thee.

PREFACE.

From the encouragement extended to our worthy publisher on the presentation of the first and second volumes of the Annual, we conclude that the experiment of 1845 may be regarded as a successful one, and the preparation of a little work of this kind an acceptable offering to the young.

The present year, our kind contributors have afforded us a much more ample supply of interesting articles than could possibly appear. We regret that any who have so generously labored for us and our young friends, should be denied the pleasure of greeting their articles on the pages of the Annual. Let them not suspect that it is from any disapproval or rejection of their labors. Be assured, dear friends, we are more grateful than can properly be expressed in a brief preface. Our warmest thanks are due our old friends, who, in the midst of other arduous duties, have willingly given us assistance. Let our new corres-pondents be assured they are gratefully remembered, although we have not the pleasure or opportunity to present their articles to our readers in the present volume. They are at the publisher's disposal for another year.

May the blessing of our Father in heaven rest upon the little book and all its mends.

M.H.A.

CONTENTS.

SMALL MEANS AND GREAT ENDS;

OR,

THE WIDOW'S POT OF OIL.

BY JULIA A. FLETCHER.

"Oh! how I do wish I was rich!" said Eliza Melvyn, dropping her work in her lap, and looking up discontentedly to her mother; "why should not I be rich as well as Clara Payson? There she passes in her father's carriage, with her fine clothes, and haughty ways; while I sit here - sew - sewing - all day long. I don't see what use I am in the world!

"Why should it be so? Why should one person have bread to waste, while another is starving? Why should one sit idle all day, while another toils all night? Why should one have so many blessings, and another so few?"

"Eliza!" said Mrs. Melvyn, taking her daughter's hand gently within her own, and pushing back the curls from her flushed brow, "my daughter, why is this? why is your usual contentment gone, and why are you so sinfully complaining? Have you forgotten to think that 'God is ever good?'"

"No, mother," replied the young girl, "but it sometimes

appears strange to me, why he allows all these things."

"Wiser people than either you or I have been led to wonder at these things," said Mrs. Melvyn; "but the Christian sees in all the wisdom of God, who allows us to be tried here, and will overrule all for our good. The very person who is envied for one blessing perhaps envies another for one he does not possess. But why would you be rich, my child?"

"Mother, I went this morning through a narrow, dirty street in another part of the city. A group of ragged children were collected round one who was crying bitterly. I made my way through them and spoke to the little boy. He told me his little sister was dead, his father was sick, and he was hungry. Here was sorrow enough for any one; but the little boy stood there with his bare feet, his sunbleached hair and tattered clothes, and smiled almost cheerfully through the tears which washed white streaks amid the darkness of his dirty face. He led me to his *home*. Oh, mother! if you had been with me up those broken stairs, and seen the helpless beings in that dismal, dirty room you would have wished, like me, for the means to help them. The dead body lay there unburied, for the man said, they had no money to pay for a coffin. He was dying himself, and they might as well be buried together."

"Are you sure, Eliza, that you have not the means to help them?" asked Mrs. Melvyn. "Put on your bonnet, my dear, and go to our sexton. Tell him to go and do what should be done. The charitable society of which I am a member will pay the expense. Then call on Dr. - the dispensary physician, and send him to the relief of the sick one. Then go to those of your acquaintance who have, as you say, 'bread to waste,' and mention to them this hungry little boy. If you have no money to give these sufferers, you have a voice to plead with those who have; and thus you may bless the poor, while you doubly bless the rich, for 'It is more blessed to give than to receive.'"

Eliza obeyed, and when she returned several hours after, her face glowing with animation, and eagerly recounted how much had been done for the poor family; how their dead had been humanely borne from their sight; how the sick man was visited by the physician, and his bitterness of spirit removed by the sympathy which was sent him; how the room was to be cleaned and ventilated, and how she left the little boy eating a huge slice of bread, while others of the family were half devouring the remainder of the loaf; her mother listened with the same gentleness. "It is well, my daughter," said she; "I preferred to send you on this errand of sympathy, that you might see how much you could do with small means."

"I have a picture here," she continued, "which I wish you to keep as a token of this day's feelings and actions. It is called 'The Widow's Pot of Oil.' Will you read me the story which belongs to it?"

Eliza took her little pocket Bible, the one that she always carried to the Sabbath school, and, turning to the fourth chapter of the second book of Kings, read the first seven verses. Turn to them now, children, and read them.

"You can see in this picture," said her mother, "how small was the 'pot of oil,' and how large were some of the vessels to be filled. Yet still it flowed on, a little stream; still knelt the widow in her faith, patiently supporting it; still brought her little sons the empty vessels; the blessing of God was upon it, and they were all filled. She feared not that the oil would cease to flow; she stopped not when one vessel was filled; she still believed, and labored, and waited, until her work was done.

"Take this picture, my daughter, and when you think that you cannot do good with small means, remember 'the widow's pot of oil,' and perseveringly use the means you have; when one labor is done, begin another; stitch by stitch you have made this beautiful garment; very large houses are built of little bricks patiently joined together one by one; and 'the widow's small pot of oil' filled many large vessels."

"Oh, mother," said Eliza, "I hope I shall never be so wicked again. I will keep the picture always. But, mother, do you not think Mr. Usher would like this picture to put in the 'Sabbath School Annual?' He might have a smaller one engraved from this, you know, and perhaps cousin Julia will write something about it. I mean to ask them."

MARY ELLEN; A SKETCH FROM LIFE.

BY MRS. MARGARET M. MASON.

"O, lightly, lightly tread!
A holy thing is sleep
On the worn spirit shed,
And eyes that wake to weep;
Ye know not what ye do,
That call the slumberer back
From the world unseen by you,
Unto life's dim faded track."

How beautiful, calm, and peaceful is sleep! Often, when I have laid my head upon my pillow happy and healthful, I have asked myself, to what shall I awaken? What changes may come ere again my head shall press this pillow? Ah, little do we know what a day may unfold to us! We know not to what we shall awaken; what joy or sorrow. I do not know when I was awakened to more painful intelligence, than when aroused one morning from pleasant dreams by the voice of a neighbor, saying that Mary Ellen, the only daughter of a near neighbor, was dying. She was a beautiful little girl, about three years of age, unlike most other children. She was more serious and thoughtful; and many predicted that her friends would not have her long. She would often ask strange questions about heaven and her heavenly Father; and many of her expressions were very beautiful.

One day she asked permission of her mother to go and gather her some flowers. Her mother gave her permission, but requested her not to go out of the field. After searching in vain for flowers, she returned with some clover leaves and blades of grass. "Mother," said she, "I could find you no flowers, but here are some spires of grass and clover leaves. Say that they are some pretty, mother. GOD made them." Often, when she woke in the morning, she would ask her mother if it was the Sabbath day. If told it was, "Then," she would say, "we will read the Bible and keep the day holy." Her mother always strove to render the Sabbath interesting to her, and to have her spend it in a profitable manner. Nor did she fail; for little Mary Ellen was always happy when the Sabbath morning came. The interest she took in the reading of the Scriptures, in explanations given of the plates in the Bible, and the accuracy with which she would remember all that was told her, were truly pleasing. Her kind and affectionate disposition, her love for all that was pure and holy, and her readiness to forgive and excuse all that she saw wrong in others, made her beloved by all who knew her. If she saw children at play on the Sabbath, or roaming about, she would notice it, and speak of it as being very wrong, and it would appear to wound her feelings; yet she would try to excuse them. "It may be," she would say, "that they do not know that it is the holy Sabbath day. Perhaps no one has told them." She could not bear to think of any one doing wrong intentionally.

Whenever she heard her little associates make use of any language that she was not quite sure was right, she would ask her mother if it was wrong to speak thus;

and if wrong, she would say, "Then, I will never speak so, and I shall be your own dear little girl, and my heavenly Father will love me." We often ask children whom they love best. Such was the question often put to Mary Ellen. She would always say, "I love my heavenly Father best, and my dear father and mother next." Her first and best affections were freely given to her Maker, not from a sense of duty alone did it seem, but from a heart overflowing with love and gratitude; and never, at the hour of retiring, would she forget to kneel and offer up her evening prayer. Thus she lived.

Now I will lead you to her dying pillow Many friends were around her. No one had told her that she was dying; yet she herself felt conscious of it. She wished to have the window raised, that she might see the ocean and trees once more. "Oh!" said her mother, bending over her, "is my dear little girl dying?" "I want to go," said Mary Ellen; "I want my father and mother to go with me." "Will you not stay with us?" said the stricken father; "will you not stay with us?" She raised her little hands and eyes - "Oh no," said she; "I see them! I see them! 't is lighter there; I want to go; get a coffin and go with me, father. 'T is lighter there!" She died soon after she ceased speaking. Her pure spirit winged its way to the blest home where we shall *all* have more light, where the mortal shall put on immortality.

She died when flowers were fading; fit season for one of so gentle and pure a nature to depart.

> "In the cold, moist earth they laid her
> When the forest cast the leaf,
> And we wept that one so beautiful
> Should have a life so brief.

And yet 't was not unmeet that one,
Like that young friend of ours,
So gentle and so beautiful,
Should perish with the flowers."

But Oh! when that little form was laid in the cold grave, - when the childless parents returned to their lonely home, once made so happy by the smile of their departed child, - Oh! who can express or describe their anguish! In her they had all they could ask in a child; she was their only one. Everything speaks to their hearts of *her*; but her light step and happy voice fall not upon their ears; to them the flowers that she loved have a mournful language. The voice of the wind sighing in the trees has to them a melancholy tone. The light laugh of little children, coming in at the open window, - the singing of birds which she delighted to hear, - but speak to their hearts of utter loneliness. They feel that the little form they had nursed with so much care and tenderness, so often pressed to their bosoms, is laid beneath the sod. Yet the sweet consolation which religion affords, cheered and sustained the afflicted parents in their hours of deepest sorrow. They would not call their child back. They feel that she has reached her heavenly home. Happy must they have been in yielding up to its Maker a spirit so pure.

Two years Mary Ellen has been sleeping in the little grave-yard. Since then another little daughter has been given her parents, - a promising little bud, that came with the spring flowers, to bless and cheer the home which was made so desolate. The best wish I have for the parents, and all I ask for the child, is, that it may be like little Mary Ellen. I have an earnest wish, too that all little children who read this sketch may be led to love and obey God as much as Mary Ellen.

THE DEAD CHILD TO ITS MOTHER.

BY MRS. E.R.B. WALDO.

Mother, mourn not for me;
No more I need of thee;
Call back the yearning which would follow where
No mortal grief can go;
All thine affection throw
Around thy living ones; they need thy care.

Let not my name still be
A word of grief to thee,
But let it bring a thought of peace and rest;
Shed for me no sad tear,
Remember, mother dear!
That I am with the perfect and the blest.

Yes, let my memory still
With joy thy bosom fill;
For, though thou dost along life's desert roam,
My spirit, like a star,
Bright burning and afar,
Shall guide thee, through the darkness, to thy home

HOPE.

BY REV. H.B. NYE.

Expectation is not desire, nor desire hope. We may *expect* misfortune, sickness, poverty, while from these evils we would fain escape. Bending over the couches of the sick and suffering, we may *desire* their restoration to health, while the hectic flush and the rapid beating of the heart assure us that no effort of kindness or skill can prolong their days upon the earth. *Hope* is directed to some future good, and it implies not only an ardent desire that our future may be fair and unclouded, but an expectation that our wishes will, at length, be granted, and our plans be crowned with large success. Hence hope animates us to exertion and diligence, and always imparts pleasure and gladness, while our fondest wishes cost us anxiety and tears.

There are *false* and *delusive* hopes, which bring us, at last, to shame. There are those who expect to gain riches by fraud and deceit, in pursuits and traffics on which the laws of truth, love, and justice, must ever darkly frown. They forget that wealth, with all its splendor, can only be deemed a good and desirable gift when sought as an instrument to advance noble and beneficent aims, - when we are the almoners of God's bounty to the lonely children of sorrow and want.

If we seek wealth, let us not forget that pure hearts gentle affections, lofty purposes, and generous deeds, can alone secure the peace and blessedness of the spiritual kingdom of God.

There are some who have a strong desire for the praise and stations of men, yet are often careless of the means by which they accomplish their ends. Remember, my young friends, that no station, no crown, or honor, will occupy the attention of a good and noble heart, except it opens a better opportunity for philanthropic labor, and is conferred as the free offering of an intelligent and grateful people.

There are many, especially among the young, who seek *present* pleasure in foolish and sinful deeds, vainly believing the wicked may flourish and receive the blessing of the good. Believe me, young friend, such hopes are delusive, and such expectations will suddenly perish. Let fools laugh and mock at sin, and live as if God were not; but consider well the path of *your* feet! When your weak arm can hold back the globes which circle in space above us in solemn grandeur and beauty forever, then may you hope to arrest the operation of those laws which preserve an everlasting connection between obedience and blessedness, sin and sorrow.

In the spring-season of life, how beautiful are the visions which Hope spreads out to our admiring view, as we go forth, with gladsome heart and step, amid the duties of life, its trials and temptations. It begets manly effort by its promises of success, and leads us to virtue and self-denial, in our weakness and sin. When our heads are bowed to the earth in despondency and gloom, hope putteth forth her hand, scattereth afar the clouds, dispelleth our sorrow; and again, with a firmer step and a more trustful heart, we go forth on the solemn march of life! It is our solace and strength in the hours of woe and grief, when those in whose smile we have rejoiced pass from our presence and homes to the valley and shadow of death. And if we weep that they are not, and can never return,

> "Hope, like the rainbow, a creature of light,
> Is born, like the rainbow, in tears,"

and we rest in the calm and blest assurance that we shall ultimately go to them, and with them dwell forever in a land without sorrow.

It may be said that we scarcely live in the present. Memory, in whose mysterious cells are treasured the records of the past, carries us back to our earlier years, and all our pursuits, and sports, and joys, and griefs, pass rapidly in review before us; and Hope leads us onward, investing future years with charms, and bidding us strive with brave and manly hearts in the conflicts and duties that remain. The former years - sorrowful remembrance! - may have been passed in luxury, indolence, or flagrant sin; the fruits of our industry and skill may have wasted away; friends, whose love once cast a golden sunshine on the path of life, may have proved false and treacherous; our fondest desires, perchance, have faded, and sorrows may encompass us about; - yet above us the voice of Hope crieth aloud, "*Press on*!" - through tears and the cross must thou win the crown; be patient, trustful, in every duty and grief; "*press on*," and falter not; and its words linger like the music of a remembered dream in our ear, until, at the borders of the grave, we lay down the burden of our sinfulness and care, and, through the open gate of death, pass onward to that world where hope shall be exchanged for sight, and we, with unveiled eye, shall look upon the wondrous ways and works of God.

THE YOUNG SOLDIER

BY REV. J.G. ADAMS.

A soldier! a soldier!
I'm longing to be;
The name and the life
Of a soldier for me!
I would not be living
At ease and at play:
True honor and glory
I'd win in my day!

A soldier! a soldier!
In armor arrayed;
My weapons in hand,
Of no contest afraid;
I'd ever be ready
To strike the first blow,
And to fight my good way
Through the ranks of the foe.

But then, let me tell you,
No blood would I shed,
No victory seek o'er
The dying and dead;
A far braver soldier
Than this would I be;
A warrior of Truth,

In the ranks of the free!

My helmet Salvation,
Strong Faith my good shield.
The sword of the Spirit
I'd learn how to wield.
And then against evil
And sin would I fight,
Assured of my triumph,
Because in the right.

A soldier! a soldier!
O, then, let me be!
Young friends, I invite you -
Enlist now with me.
Truth's bands will be mustered -
Love's foes shall give way!
Let's up, and be clad
In our battle array!

THE STOLEN CHILDREN.

BY MRS. M.A. LIVERMORE.

Not many years ago, the beautiful hills and valleys of New England gave to the wild Indian a home, and its bright waters and quiet forests furnished him with food. Rude wigwams stood where now ascends the hum of the populous city, and council-fires blazed amid the giant trees which have since bowed before the axe of the settler. Between that rude age and the refinement of the present day, many and fearful were the strifes of the red owner of the land with the invading white man, who, having crossed the waters of the Atlantic, sought to drive him from his hitherto undisputed possessions. The recital of deeds of inhuman cruelty which characterized that period; the rehearsal of bloody massacres of inoffensive women and innocent children, which those cruel savages delighted in, would even now curdle the blood with horror, and make one sick at heart.

It was in this period of fearful warfare that the events occurred which form the foundation of the following story.

Not far from the year 1680, a small colony was planted on the banks of the beautiful Connecticut. A little company from the sea-side found their way, through the tangled and pathless woods, to the meadows that lay sleeping on the banks of this bright river; and here, after having felled the mighty trees whose brows had long been kissed by the pure heavens, they erected their humble cottages; and began to till the rich alluvial soil. The colonists were persevering and industrious; and soon a little village grew up beside the shining stream, fields of Indian corn waved their wealth of tasselled heads in the breezes, the rudely-constructed school-house echoed with the cheerful hum of the little students, and a rustic church was dedicated to the God of the Pilgrims. He who officiated as the spiritual teacher of this new parish, also instructed the children during the week. A man he was of no inferior mind, or neglected education; of fervent, but austere piety, possessing a bold spirit and a benevolent heart. His family consisted of a wife and two daughters; Emma, the elder, was a girl of eight summers, and Anna, the younger, was about five.

Never were children so frolicsome and mirth-loving as were Emma and Anna Wilson, the daughters of the minister. Not the grave admonitions of their mother, or the severe reproofs of their stern father; not their many confinements in dark and windowless closets, or the memory of afternoons, when, supperless, they had been sent to bed while the sun was yet high in the heavens; not the fear of certain punishment, or the suasion of kindness, could tame their wild natures, or force them into anything like woman-like sobriety. Hand in hand, they would wander amid the aisles of mossy-trunked trees, plucking the flowers that carpeted the earth; now digging for ground-nuts, now turning over the leaves for acorns; sometimes they would watch the nibbling squirrel as he nimbly sprang from tree to tree, or overpower, with their boisterous laughter, the gushing melody of the bobolink; they mocked the querulous cat-bird and the cawing crow, started at the swift winging of the shy blackbird, and stood still to listen to the sweet song of the clear-throated thrush; now they bathed their feet in the streamlets that went singing on their way to the Connecticut, and then, throwing up handfuls of the running water, which fell again upon their heads, they laughed right merrily at their self-baptism. They were happy as the days were long; but wild as their playfellows, the birds, the streams, and the squirrels.

One beautiful Sabbath morning in July, their mother dressed them tidily in their best frocks, and tying on their snow-white sun-bonnets, she sent them to church nearly an hour before she started with their father, that they might walk leisurely, and have opportunity to get rested before the commencement of services. But it was not until near the middle of the sermon that the little rogues made their appearance. Withglowing faces, hair that had strayed from its ungraceful confinement to float in golden curls over their necks and shoulders, - with bonnets, shoes and stockings tied together and swinging over each arm, - with dresses rent, ripped, soiled and stained, and up-gathered aprons filled with berries, blossoms, pebbles, fresh-water shells and bright sand, they stole softly to where their mother was sitting, much to her mortification, and greatly to the horror of their pious father.

For this offence, they were forbidden to accompany their parents, on the next Sabbath, to church, but were condemned to close confinement in the house during the long, bright, summer day - a severer punishment than which, could not have been inflicted. When the hour of assembling for worship was announced by the old English clock that stood in the corner, the curtains were drawn before the windows; two bowls of bread and milk were placed on the dresser for their dinner; a lesson in the Testament was assigned to Emma, and one in the Catechism to Anna; a strict injunction to remain all day in the house was laid upon both, and Mr. and Mrs. Wilson departed, locking the door, and taking the key. The children soon wiped away the tears that their hard fate had gathered in their eyes, and applied themselves to their tasks, which were speedily committed. Then the forenoon wore slowly away; they dared not get their playthings, - they were forbidden to go out doors, - and the only books in the room were the Bible, Watts' Hymns, and the Pilgrim's Progress, which lay on the highest shelf in the room, far beyond their reach. Noon came at last; the sun shone fully in at the south window, betokening the dinner hour, and then their dinner of bread and milk was eaten. What were they next to do? Sorrowfully they gazed on the smiling river, the green corn-fields, the large potato-plats, the grazing cattle, the blooming flower-beds, and the shady walks which led far into the cool recesses of the forest; and earnestly did they long for liberty to ramble out in the glorious sunshine. As they were gazing wistfully through the window, they saw their playful little kitten, Fanny, dart like lightning from her hiding-place in the garden, where she had long lain in ambush, and fasten her sharp claws in the back of a poor little ground-bird, which had been hopping from twig to twig, chirping and twittering very cheerfully. The little bird fluttered, gasped, and uttered wailing cries, as it ineffectually labored to free itself from the power of its captor, until Emma and Anna, unable longer to witness its distress, sprang out the window, and, rushing down the garden, liberated the little prisoner, and with delight saw it fly away towards the woods.

Delighted to find themselves once more in the open air, the joyful children forgot the prohibition of their parents, and leaping over the dear little brook with which they loved to run races, they filled their aprons with the blue-eyed violets that grew on its margin. On they bounded, further and further, and a few moments more found them in the dense wood, where not a sunbeam could reach the ground. But suddenly the leaves rustled behind them, and the twigs cracked, and there sprung, from an ambuscade in the thicket, the tall figure of an Indian, who laid a strong hand on the arm of each little girl, and, despite the cries, tears, and entreaties of the poor children, hurried them deeper into the forest, where they found a large body of these cruel savages, clad in moose and deer skins, armed with bows and arrows, tomahawks, and muskets. The children were questioned concerning the village, the occupation of the inhabitants on that day, and the number of men at home, and they replied correctly and intelligibly. A consultation was then held among the Indians, which resulted in a determination to attack the village; and forthwith, leaving but one behind to guard the little prisoners, they made a descent on the quiet settlement, burning and ravaging buildings on their way to the church. But they did not find the body of worshippers unarmed, as they doubtless expected; for, in those days of peril and savage warfare, men worshipped God armed with musket and bayonet, and the hand that was lifted in prayer to heaven would often, at the next moment, draw the gleaming sword from its sheath. At the meeting-house, the savages met with a warm repulse; and were so surprised and affrighted that they retreated back into the wild woods, after wounding but one or two colonists, among whom was Mr. Wilson, Emma's and Anna's father.

The Indians commenced, about dark, a journey to the settlement where they belonged, taking the stolen children with them; they reached their destination early on the second day of their travel. Rough, indeed, seemed the Indian village to the white children: the houses were only wigwams, made by placing poles obliquely in the ground, and fastening them at the top, covered on the outside with bark, and lined on the inside with mats; some containing but one family, others a great many. The furniture consisted of mats for beds, curiously wrought baskets to hold corn, and strings of wampum which served for ornaments. Into one of the smallest of these wigwams Emma and Anna were carried, and were given to the wife of one of the chief warriors, who had but one child of her own, - Winona was her name, which signifies the first-born, - a bright-eyed, pleasant, winning little girl of two years of age. The mother scrutinized them closely, but the child appeared overjoyed to see them, and wiped away their tears with her little hand, and, jabbering in her unknown language, seemed begging them not to cry. This interested the mother, and she soon looked more kindly upon them, and set before them food. But they were too sorrowful to eat, and were glad to be shown a mat, where they were to sleep. Locked in each others' arms, cheek pressed to cheek, they lay and wept as if their hearts were broken.

"Let us pray to God," whispered Emma, after the inmates of the wigwam were reposing in slumber, "and ask Him to bring us again to our father and mother."

So they rose, and knelt in the dark wigwam, with their arms about one another's necks, and their tears flowing together, and offered to God their childish prayer:

"Our Father in Heaven, love us poor children; take care of us; forgive us for doing wrong, and help us be good; take care of our dear parents; comfort them, and bring us again to meet them."

Then, more composed, and trusting in the blessed Father of us all, they fell asleep, and sweet were their slumbers, though far from their dear parents and home, for angels watched over them, and gave to them happy dreams.

A few days' residence among these untutored red men made Emma and Anna great favorites among them; their pleasant dispositions, their good nature, and, above all, their love for the little Winona, which was fully reciprocated, endeared them to the father and mother of the Indian girl. Though sad at being separated from their parents, and though they often wept until they could weep no longer when they thought of home, yet their hearts, like those of all children, were easily consoled, and their spirits were so elastic that they could not long be depressed. Winona loved them tenderly; at night she slept between them, and during the day she would never leave them. She wore garlands of their wreathing, listened to their English songs, stroked their rosy cheeks, and frolicked with them in the woods, and beside the running brooks.

Two months passed away; all the Indian women in the village were speaking of the love that had sprung up between the little white girls and the copper-colored Winona; and many a hard hand smoothed the golden curls of the little captives in token of affection. Then Winona was taken sick; her body glowed with the fever-heat, her bright eyes became dull, and day and night she moaned with pain. With surprising care and tenderness, Emma and Anna nursed the suffering child, - for to them were her glowing and burning hands extended for relief, rather than to her mother. They held her throbbing head, lulled her to sleep, bathed her hot temples, moistened her parched lips, and soothed her distresses; but they could not win her from the power of death - and she died!

Oh, it was a sorrowful thing to them to part with their little playmate, - to see the damp earth heaped upon her lovely form, and to feel that she was forever hidden from their sight! They wept, and, with the almost frantic mother, laid their faces on the tiny grave, and moistened it with their tears. Hither they often came to scatter the freshest flowers, and to weep for the home they feared they would never again see; and here they often kneeled in united prayer to that God, who bends on prayerful children a loving eye, and spreads over them a shadowing wing.

The childless Indian woman now loved them more than ever; but the death of Winona had opened afresh the fountains of their grief, and often did she find them weeping so bitterly that she could not comfort them. She would draw them to her bosom, and tenderly caress them; but it all availed not, and when the month of October came, with its sere foliage and fading flowers, Emma and Anna had grown so thin, and pale, and feeble, from their wearing home-sickness, that they stayed all day in the wigwam, going out only to visit Winona's grave. They drooped and drooped, and those who saw them said, "The white children will die, and lie down with Winona."

The Indian mother gazed on their pallid faces, and wept; she loved them, and could not bear to part with them; but she saw they would die, and calling her husband, she bade him convey them to the home of their father. Many were the tears she shed at parting with them; and when they disappeared among the thick trees, she threw herself, in an agony of grief, upon the mats within the wigwam.

It was Sabbath noon when the children arrived in sight of their father's house; here the Indian left them, and plunged again into the depths of the forest. They could gain no admittance into the house, and they hastened to the meeting-house, where they hoped to find their parents. They reached the church; the congregation was singing; silently, and unobserved, they entered, and seated themselves at the remotest part of the building. The singing ceased; there was a momentary pause, and their father rose before them. Oh, how he was changed! Pale, very pale, thin and sad was his dear face; and Emma's and Anna's hearts smote them, as being the cause of this change. They leaned forward to catch a glimpse of their mother, but in her accustomed seat sat a lady dressed in black, and this, they thought, could not be her; they little supposed that their parents mourned for them as for the dead, believing they should see them no more.

Mr. Wilson took his text from Psalms: "It is good for me that I have been afflicted." With a tremulous voice, he spoke of their recent afflictions; of the sudden invasion of the colony, the burning of their dwellings, the wounding of some of their number, and then his tones became more deeply tremulous, for he spoke of his children. The sobs of his sympathizing people filled the house, and the anguish of the father's feelings became so intense, that he bowed his head upon the Bible and wept aloud. The hearts of the children palpitated with emotion; their sobs arose above all others; and, taking each other by the hand, the wan, emaciated, badly-dressed little girls hastened to the pulpit, where stood their father, with his face bowed upon the leaves of the Holy Book, and laying their hand upon his passive arm, they sobbed forth, "Father! Father!" He raised his head, gazed eagerly and wildly upon the children, and comprehending at once the whole scene, the revulsion of feeling that came over him was so great, - the sorrow for the dead being instantly changed into joy for the living, - that he staggered backwards, and would have fallen but for the timely support of a chair.

The whole house was in instant confusion; in a moment they were clasped in their mother's arms, and kisses and tears and blessings were mingled together upon their white, thin cheeks. "Let us thank God for the return of our children," said the pastor; and all kneeling reverently, he thanked our merciful heavenly Father, in the warm and glowing language of a deeply grateful heart, for restoring to his arms those whom he had wept as lost to him forever.

Oh, there was joy in that village that night again and again the children told their interesting story, and those who listened forgot to chide their disobedience, or to harshly reprove. Need I tell you how they were pressed to the bosoms of the villagers; how tears were shed for their sufferings, and those of the little lost Winona, whom they did not forget; how caresses were lavished upon them, and prayers offered to God, that their lives, which he had so wonderfully preserved, might be spent in usefulness and piety? No, I need not, for you can imagine it all.

The sermon which was so happily interrupted by the return of the children was the first Mr. Wilson had attempted to preach since the day they were stolen; the wounds he that day received, and the illness that immediately afterwards ensued, with his unutterable grief for the loss of his children, had confined him mostly to his bed during theirabsence. On the next Sabbath, Emma and Anna accompanied their father and mother once more to church, when Mr. Wilson preached from these words: "Oh, give thanks unto the Lord, for he is good, and his mercy endureth forever."

MY GRANDMOTHER'S COTTAGE.

BY REV. J.G. ADAMS.

Of all places in the wide world, my own early home excepted, none seem to me more pleasing in memory than my grandmother's cottage. Very often did I visit it in my boyhood, and well acquainted with its appearance within, and with almost every object around it, did I become. It stood in a quiet nook in the midst of the woods, about five miles from the pleasant seaport where I was born. The cottage was not a spacious one. It had but few rooms in it; but it was amply large for my aged grandparents, I remember. They lived happily there. My grandfather was somewhat infirm; my grandmother was a very vigorous person for one of seventy-five; this was her age at the time of my first recollection of her. She used to walk from her cottage to our home; and once I walked with her, but was exceedingly mortified that I could not endure the walk so well as she did.

I used to love this cottage home, because it was so quiet, and in the summer time so delighting to me. I believe I received some of my very first lessons in the love of nature in this place. It was a charming summer or winter retreat. If the sun shone warmly down anywhere, it was here. If the wind blew kindly anywhere, it was around the snug cottage, sheltered as it was on every side by the tall old pines. If the robin's note came earliest anywhere in the spring-time, it was from the large spreading apple-tree just at the foot of the little garden lot. How often has my young heart been delighted with his song there! And then, what sweet chanting I have heard in those woods all the day from the thrush and sparrow, yellow-bird and oriole! How their mellow voices would seem to echo in the noon-silence, or at the sunset hour, as though they were singing anthems in some vast cathedral! They were; and what anthems of nature's harmony and praise! God heard them, and was glorified.

It seemed to me that every animate thing was made to be happy. I loved to stand beneath a tall old hemlock in a certain part of the wood, and watch the squirrels as they skipped and ran so swiftly along the wall, or from branch to branch, or up and down the trees. Their chattering made a fine accompaniment to the bird-songs. And here I learned to indulge a fondness for the very crows, which to this day I have never outgrown. Though they have been denounced as mischievous, and bounties have been set upon them, I never could find it in my heart to indulge in the warring propensity against them. They always seemed to me such social company - issuing from some edge of the woodland, and slowly flapping their black wings, and flocking out into the clearing, huddling overhead, and sailing away, chatting so loudly and heartily all the while, and reminding the whole neighborhood that when we have life, it is best to let others know it! Yes - the cawing crows have been company for me in many a solitary ramble; and whenever I hear them, I inwardly pay my respects to them. All these, and other familiar sights and sounds, did I richly enjoy at the old cottage in the woods.

I loved to sit at the shed-door, and watch my grandfather at his slow work; for he had been a mechanic in his day, and was able to do a little very moderately at his trade now. He would tell me the history of the old people in the neighborhood, and of the customs and fashions when they were boys and girls; and my eyes and ears were open to hear him. I used to wish I could see them just as they looked when they were children. It was very difficult then for me to imagine how those who had become so wrinkled could ever have had the smooth faces of infants and children. But my grandfather could remember when he was a boy; and his father had told him what things were done when he, too, was a boy. And so I concluded that wrinkles were no disgrace, nor the fairest faces of the young any protection against them.

My grandmother was very fond of me, and took great pleasure in having me read to her, as her eyesight had become somewhat dim. And so I used to load myself with story-books and newspapers, when I became older, to carry and read to her. And such times as we had with them! Voyages, travels, discoveries, adventures, perils, - the wonders of the world, the wonders of science, the wonders of history, - all came in for their share of reading. Though I should read myself tired and sleepy, my grandmother would still be an interested listener. Since I have been a minister, I have often wished that many hearers would as eagerly listen to what I had to say especially to them, as did my aged grandmother to my young words then.

Those sunny days have departed. The old cottage is not there now. Years ago it was taken down. My grandfather died when I was yet a boy, and I followed him to the grave with a heavy heart. My grandmother lived to be almost a hundred years old, - her powers all gone, and she helpless. It would sometimes, even in my manhood, deeply affect me to have her look into my face with no sign in hers that she knew me, when she had once loved her talkative and delighted grandchild so fondly. But she, too, found her resting-place at last beside her companion. Peace to them! They blest me with their kindly, cheering words when most I needed them, and I will bless their memories. And peace to the spot where once stood their quiet home! Wherever in life I may be, - however brightly its pleasures may shine, or heavily its cares and afflictions press upon me - never would I outgrow the inspiration of these early enjoyments; never forget, that, however the great, proud, and contentious world may distract and dishearten, there will yet be peace to the humble and virtuous soul in many a nook like that which sheltered and blest my grand mother's cottage.

THE FIRST OATH

BY REV. EBEN FRANCIS.

It is now many years since a near friend of mine uttered his first oath. We were very intimate in our youthful days. I have thought that I would write a little story about him, for some of the little folks of these times to read, hoping that it will not only be interesting, but do them good; for I am indeed sorry to know that swearing is a very common sin among the boys of our times.

The parents of my young playfellow were of the humbler class in society; they were industrious and prudent, and took great pains to teach him what was right. They lived in the metropolis of New England, where my schoolmate was born. His father wrought with the saw, the plane, the hammer, and such tools as carpenters use about their business. His home was a neat, wooden two-story house, in one of the streets of that part of Boston which was generally known, when we were boys, by the name of the MILL-POND. I suppose that most of my little readers who live in the city can tell where it is. Many changes have taken place there since my childhood. When I was a small boy it was called the *town*, - now we never hear of it but as the *city* of Boston. Its population has increased rapidly; its territory has been extended; it has grown in wealth, in splendor, in its means for mental and moral improvement; in the number and convenience of its public schools, - the pride and ornament, or the disgrace, of any place. Yes, Boston is not, in appearance or in fact, what it once was.

But I am getting off from my story. I was saying that my young friend resided on the "new-land" - no; the "Mill-Pond;" - well, it's all the same - for when they dug down old Beacon Hill, they threw the dirt into the Mill-Pond, and when it was filled up, or made land, the spot was still known as the Mill-Pond, and oftentimes was called the new-land. In later years, there have been other portions added to the city, by making wharves, and filling up where the tide used to ebb and flow, and where large vessels could float.

But again I am digressing too far from the story.

So soon as my friend was old enough, he was sent to one of the primary schools, and was a pretty constant scholar at that, and afterwards at a grammar school, till he was about twelve years old. He was, of course, much with other lads of his own age, and some who were older and younger than himself. He was, also, often in the streets, and as there were a great many people who used profane language in those days, - as there are at the present time, - he heard much of it; yet he had been so carefully trained that he did not for years utter wicked words.

It is always painful to most persons, old as well as young, to hear profanity, even though it be very common in their hearing, if they are never accustomed to its use.

My young friend had been taught to reverence the name of that great Being who made heaven and earth and all things. He was a member of a Sabbath school, and thus had much valuable advice from his faithful teacher to govern his conduct in word and deed. For a while he heeded this, and was careful of his moral character. But by-and-by, he overstepped the bounds of right.

It is very true that "evil communications corrupt good manners;" and that if one would not be bad, one means of safety is to keep out of bad company.

My friend was, in a few years, placed in a store, where there was a large business carried on. He came in contact with persons who were not so carefully instructed as he had been. They made no hesitation in pronouncing the names of God and Jesus Christ in a blasphemous and profane manner. He resisted the pernicious influence of their example for a while, but at last it became so familiar to his ears, that he could hear wicked words spoken without even a thrill of horror in his bosom.

He, however, had not the disposition to speak them, till one day, when some little thing in the store did not suit him, his passion was aroused, and, in the angry excitement of the moment, he spoke out, - and in that unguarded expression there was profanity, - a miserable, blasphemous, wicked word. He had uttered his *first oath.* The disposition had been lurking in his heart for several days to do this; but he had not been able to so far lower his moral sense as to do it before. Now he felt as though he had done a brave act, - that he had achieved something very grand. But soon, very soon, conscience whispered her gentle yet severe rebuke. She complained sadly of the wickedness that was done. The blush of shame mantled his cheek. Remorse took hold on his spirit. He looked about to see who was upbraiding him; but none seemed to notice it. He resolved that he would not again give occasion for such feelings of regret and sorrow to himself as he then felt.

Could you have then looked into his heart, you would have pitied him. This resolution he kept a few weeks, when, being a little irritated, he a second time profaned the holy name of Deity. This time he felt some compunctions of conscience, but they were not as powerful as before; the first step had been already taken, and a second was much easier.

I need not go on to tell you how he, not long after, broke a second resolution, and so on, till, ere many months, he had become really a swearing young man.

It all sprang from the first sinful act; and when at last he did break himself of the habit, it was not done without a serious struggle.

I have told you this story, my young readers, because I thought it might be, not only interesting to you, but because I hoped it might be the means of leading you to reflect upon the uselessness and wickedness of PROFANITY; and that it might aid in impressing on your minds the importance of governing your passions and keeping your tongues free from evil speaking.

I see my friend, about whom I have written, quite often. He is now a parent, and occupies an eminent position in the community; but he often thinks of his former life, and says he has not yet ceased to lament his FIRST OATH. Let this fact, then, teach you how a recollection of the sins of boyhood, even though you may call them little sins, will be cherished through life, and poison many moments that would otherwise be happy ones. How important that childhood be pure and righteous in the sight of God, and to our own consciences, in order to insure a happy manhood and old age!

THE FAIRY'S GIFT.

BY REV. J. WESLEY HANSON.

It was a quiet summer's day,
The breeze blew cool and fair,
And blest ten thousand happy things
Of land, and sea, and air,
And played a thousand merry pranks
With MARY'S golden hair.

MARY was not a happy girl;
Her face was sad and sour,
And on her little pretty brow
Dark frowns did often lower, -
And she would scold, and fret, and cry,
Full fifty times an hour.

She sat and wept with grief and pain,
And did not smile at all, -
And when her friends and mates came near
She shunned them, great and small, -
And then upon the Fairy Queen
She earnestly did call.

"Oh, hither, hither, good Fairy,
I pray thee come to me!
And point me out the Path of Peace,
That I may happy be,

For I cannot, in all the world,
A moment's pleasure see!

"I try my work, my play I try,
My little playmates, too;
Help me to find true happiness,
I sadly, humbly sue; -
Oh! my lot is a darksome one, -
Fairy! what shall I do?"

A humble-bee comes riding by,
No bigger than my thumb,
And on his browny, gold-striped back,
Behold the Fairy come!
One look upon her loveliness
Makes little MARY dumb.

She wore a veil of gossamer,
Her tunic was of blue,
A golden sunbeam was her belt,
And bonnet of crimson hue,
And through the net of her purple shawl
Clear silver stars looked through.

Her slippers were of sunflower seeds,
And tied with spider's thread,
A rein of silkworm's finest yarn
Passed round the bee's brown head;
An oaten straw was her riding whip, -
Oh how her courser sped!

She beckoned to the sighing maid,
And led her a little way,
And showed a hundred fountains bright
That bubbled night and day,
And flashed their waves in the glad sunlight,

And showers of crystal spray.

She said: "Each stream has secret power
Upon the human heart,
And, as you drink, the mystic draught
Shall joy or woe impart;
'T will give you pleasant happiness,
Or sorrow's painful smart."

The founts were labelled every one,
With titles plainly seen, -
The fountains *Pride*, and *Sin*, and *Wrong*,
And *Hate*, and *Scorn*, and *Spleen,*
Goodness and *Love*, and many more,
Sparkled along the green.

And MARY drank at each bright fount,
To draw her grief away;
But, spite of all the water's power,
Her sorrows they would stay.
And still she mourned, and still was sad,
Through all the livelong day.

One morn she saw a little spring
She never saw before,
Down in a still and shady vale,
Covered with blossoms o'er, -
And when she 'd drunk, and still would drink
She thirsted still for more.

She gladly quaffed its cooling draught,
And found what she had sought;
No more her heart with sorrow grieved.
She thirsted now for nought;
She'd found a blessed happiness,
Beyond her highest thought.

And when she moved the vines aside
That hid the fount from sight,
In loveliest, brightest characters,
Like stars of silver light, -
Goodness of heart, and speech, and life,
She read in letters bright.

And MARY drank the liquid waves,
And soon her little brow
Became as pure, and clear, and white,
As bank of whitest snow;
And when she drank of that blest fount,
She purest joy did know.

Then MARY learned this highest truth.
Beyond all human art, -
That there are many things in life
Can pain and woe impart; -
But Goodness alone of act and deed
Can make a happy heart.

A LESSON TAUGHT BY NATURE.

BY MISS LOUISA M. BARKER.

When I was a little child, younger than those for whom this book is written, my home was in a valley. The usual appendages to a farm-house, the garden, orchard and small pasture grounds, lay very near it; and I was as familiar with these enclosures as with the rooms of the house. A little further off there was a mimic river, which, as it wound about, divided itself into different streams, and surrounded little islands, shaded with the tall plane tree and the flexible willow. Here, too, with those who were old enough to be careful in crossing the rustic bridges, I sometimes played on summer afternoons; - gathered the prettiest flowers in the sweetest little woods, and dipped my feet into the clear running water.

Beyond these there lay less frequented fields, which rose gradually, at no very great distance, into a range of hills as green as the valley below. One of them was covered all over its summit, and a little way down its sides, with some dark old woods. The trees which grew there were very tall, and so large that their thick and heavy tops seemed to crowd together, so that you might have walked on them almost as well as upon the hill itself. I loved sometimes, when the air was full of the bright sunshine, to look at the rich shades of green upon those tree-tops; but if ever my eye rested, for a moment only, upon the dark and mysterious avenues which led into the depths of the wood beneath them, there would creep such a chill to my heart, - such a feeling of dread would come over me, - that I turned quickly to the glad-looking homestead, that I might again grow warm and happy.

At first it was probably no more than the idea that those woods formed a limit to the world of light and gladness in which I lived. My eye could not penetrate their dimness, and with a childish, human feeling I shrank from the undiscovered and unknown. But as I grew older, and read the stories in the small books which were given to me for presents, or lent by my little friends, I had other and plainer reasons for the apprehensive feeling with which I looked at the woods. I found that children had been so lost among their thickets as hardly to be found again; and that two poor little orphans, left there on purpose, had lain down and died of hunger and weariness; and the birds covered them over with leaves. Strange birds I thought there were in the woods. Then the fairies that dwelt there, and the strange elfin creatures, and the perils that travellers fell into with robbers and wild beasts; and still I referred the scene of every story I read directly to those very woods upon the hill-side, although they were so near that I could see them plainly enough from the windows of the cheerful rooms at home.

Time passed along in its usual way; but before I had acquired knowledge or strength of mind enough to correct my early impressions of the woods, I had permission, one bright afternoon in June, to go with an older sister to a strawberry meadow across the creek. We were accompanied by some little maidens, who were older and more adventurous than me; and so it happened that when we did not find the fruit so abundant as we could wish, they persuaded us to go into another field, and then into another, I little thought where, until I became suddenly sensible of a shaded light around me, of a breeze a little cooler than that which tempered the warm air of the valley, and a low, wild music that I had never heard before; and looking up, I saw that we were actually upon the ascent of the hill which led up to the dreaded woods.

Strange and almost horror-struck as I felt, I did not scream out, (perhaps I should not have had breath to do so,) but I gathered up all the wisdom that my little heart could boast, into the resolution not to look at the woods, not to think of them; for we should soon go back again, I thought, and nothing would happen. And my young friends can judge how terrified I must have grown, when I heard one of the girls begin to talk of the beautiful flowers her brother had brought her from the woods, and end by proposing that we should go there, and get some for ourselves. I waited breathlessly to hear the objections which I doubted not would be urged against this plan, but none were offered; and when I ventured to remonstrate, they paid so little attention to me, that my pride was hurt at the thought of saying any more.

There was another way in which my pride was at work. I was ashamed, among those who were so brave, to own that I was afraid; so, though I held the hands of those who led me pretty tight, and gave them some little trouble to pull me along, they knew nothing more of my reluctance to go with them.

We got up the hill very fast; so at least it seemed to

me. Here and there a solitary tree, a few feet in advance, looked as if it had stepped out to welcome and encourage us to pass on; and I cannot say that my strength did not revive a little as I passed under the heavy branches, and out again into the freer air. Be that as it may, it was terrible enough to me, the approach to those woods. My companions were eager and gay, and shouted out, as we entered them. They little thought how overpowering were my feelings. And I little thought, myself, that I was then and there to receive a lesson that I should never forget; one, perhaps, that would do me more good than any other that I should ever learn.

At first, I was so frightened that my senses were all in confusion; but as I gradually recovered the use of them, I took notice of the coolness and the shade, and the dimness away in the distance; I heard the leafy murmur above my head, the sweet notes that the birds were singing, and the loud echoes. All these things seemed to blend together into something so solemn and so magnificent, that I began to feel for the first time what it was to be a little child. With that, soon came a feeling of confidence and even love. I thought that the majestic presence that filled the woods, whatever it was, would not hurt me, and my heart grew so light at the thought, that I began to gather flowers with the rest. How pretty they were! and what clean, shining leaves! And here and there, wherever a little sunshine found an opening in the branches and streamed down upon the bright green moss, it seemed so golden, so clear, and so real, just as if I might clasp it in my hands!

I grew so much affected, at length, that I sobbed myself into tears, and my sister said that I had never been in the woods before, and she would take me home. I did not like to say that I wanted to stay longer, but held to my flowers; and after I reached home, was washed and rested, I went to the window, and remained there a long time, looking at the woods. I did not quite comprehend all I had thought and felt, but it seemed to me that a great truth, one that would do me good, had dawned upon my mind.

It was a long time before I fully understood the lesson. In a few weeks I caught one of those contagious diseases which children must have once; and it went so hard with me, that, before I was able to walk about, and go out of the house, the leaves were all gone, and the snow had covered the ground. When spring returned I thought often of the woods, but I was too sickly to go there; and when I grew strong again, my thoughts were all occupied with an approaching event. Several changes had occurred in the family, and others were expected, to which my friends though discontented at first, had grown quite reconciled. It was not so with me. There was one circumstance which affected me more than it did others, and from that I prophesied a continual succession of evils. It seemed to me that my life was to be wholly changed, and all the joy and beauty left behind. It was childish, I know. I knew it then, for I would not for the world have told any one how I felt. Still I was as much affected by it as I have ever been since at any real grief.

Late one afternoon, when my thoughts were busy with my fears, I went to the window, and looked up at the woods. The sunshine was very bright on their tops, and the shadow very dark on the hill-side below. Very vividly then came back to me the memory of my visit to them the year before. I thought of the evils which I expected to meet, and of the beauty which I found there. It was some good angel which whispered then in my thoughts, that, just as I went to the woods, full of fears and forebodings, I was approaching the expected misfortune; that I might be as happily disappointed in this as I had been in that.

I cannot tell how delighted I was with this suggestion, nor how completely it took possession of my mind. I was gloomy and fearful no longer. I did not, indeed, when the change came, resign what I lost by it without regret; but I was so certain of finding new enjoyments, that I resigned it cheerfully. And when, after a few weeks' experience had taught me that many advantages and many pleasures had come to me in consequence of those very circumstances which I had dreaded so much, I bound the lesson of the woods to my heart so firmly that there it still remains.

And let me say to you, for whom I have related this little incident of my childhood: - do not tremble at the disappointments and trials which await you. Do not seek to throw upon others any part of them which you may more becomingly bear yourself. If you live always in the open sunshine, you will never know what beauty there is in the woods. You will find the sentiment in your books, that it is the night-time only that shows us the stars; and in the gloom which must sometimes fall upon this uncertain and mortal life of ours, you may find, if you will, as much to rejoice in as to dread. You will form plans, and indulge in hopes, which cannot be realized, and disappointment will look frowningly upon you; but if you will submit yourself to the trial like a little child, the hand that will lead you through it will point you to happier scenes than those of your own imagining.

You will have friends to love, that death may take away from you - and, oh! then, the shadow of the woodland, as it lies against the sunny meadow, will be less dark than your life. But do not despair. The few rays of light that reach you will be richer, the flowers will be purer, and the music will be softer and sweeter; for you will be nearer heaven than you were before.

There is another shadow which you and I, and all of us, are approaching, - "the shadow of death." But will not "the lesson" brighten our approach even to that? Certain I am, that if *that* hour of my childhood, when, with a fearful heart, I went into the solemn woods, and heard the sweet singing of the bird and the breeze, shall be remembered then, even though the light of life be fading away, "I shall fear no evil."

FLORENCE DREW.

"I will not go to Sabbath school to-morrow," said Florence Drew, as she threw aside her catechism and sat herself sullenly by the window.

"Florence!" said her mother; "I am astonished to hear you speak so rashly."

"I don't care, - I will not go, - my lesson is so hard I can't get it;" saying which, she burst into tears. Mrs. Drew cast a look of sorrow upon her only child as she left her to regain her good humor.

No sooner had the door closed after her mother than the rustling of leaves beneath the window drew the attention of Florence. Thinking it her favorite Carlo, and being in no mood for a frolic, without lifting her eyes she bid him "begone;" but she was soon undeceived by a shrill voice pronouncing her name, at the same time finding her arm tightly grasped by the thin, bony fingers of Crazy Nell, the terror of all the truant children in the village. The terrified child vainly tried to disengage herself from the maniac's hold; and, finding her calls for help all unheeded, she gave up in despair.

The wild, searching eyes of Crazy Nell detected her terror, and her stern features relaxed into a smile as she said, "Poor child! I will not harm you; you fear me, and think me mad; yes, I have been mad, but I'm not now; and I have come to save you from being as I have been. Nay, Florence, 't is useless for you to try to escape me; I will detain you but a short time. I heard your angry words as I was gathering herbs, and saw you fling your book away. I heard all. Listen to me, Florence Drew, and I will tell you a story by which I hope you will profit.

"I was once young, gay, and happy, as you, and, like you, an only and indulged, but wilful child, with a quick and ungoverned temper.

"One day, I was studying my Sabbath school lesson, and finding it, as I thought, rather hard, I threw it away, as you did yours, saying that I would not go to school at all. My poor mother's entreaties were all unheeded by me, and I grew up in idleness and ignorance. My mother's health daily declined, partly through my ill-treatment and wickedness. Often did she plead with me, with tears streaming down her cheeks, to alter my conduct; but I rudely repulsed her."

Nell paused, and seemed very much agitated; her eyes glared wildly, and bending close to Florence, she continued in a whisper: "We became very poor, in consequence of my extravagance; I then thought my mother a burden; she was too ill to work, and I left her to starve; she did not, however; she died of a broken heart. *I was her murderer*! 'T was that which drove me mad. Look! see you not that black cloud which darkens the sunshine of my life?"

"I cannot see a cloud," sobbed poor Florence, who was now tasting the bitter cup of repentance.

"I know it, poor child!" continued Nell; "the cloud I mean is such as you just felt, - Temper. *It is within us*! Conquer your temper, Florence Drew, and you may yet be good and happy. Go, now, and seek mother, who is at this moment shedding tears of sorrow for her little girl's ill-temper. Go to her and - " But, ere she could finish, Florence had glided into her mother's room, and was kneeling humbly at her feet Tears of sorrow were changed to those of joy and repentance, as Mrs. Drew folded her little girl to her breast in a long and affectionate embrace.

Florence has never been unkind to her mother, or given freedom to her temper, since that day. She is now the teacher of a class in a Sabbath school, and she often relates to her little scholars the story I have just related to you.

Crazy Nell continues to gather herbs, an object of pity to the benevolent, and of sport to the unfeeling. And now, my dear little readers, I must repeat Crazy Nell's expression: "Conquer your temper, and you will be happy;" or, in the words of the sacred Scriptures, "He that ruleth his own spirit is greater than he that taketh a city."

MAY.

SHECHEM.

BY REV. J.G. ADAMS.

In the picture opposite, the reader will see represented a part of the city of Shechem, at the foot of Mount Gerizim. It is a very noted place in history. It is called Sychar in the Gospel, John 4:5. It was here, at Jacob's well, that Jesus met the woman of Samaria. The account of the conversation which they held together is one of the most interesting records in the New Testament. I wish all our young readers would make themselves acquainted with it. Jesus was a Jew; and the Jews had no dealings with the Samaritans. Weary with travelling in the heat of the day, our Lord sat down to rest by that ancient well, when the stranger woman came to draw water from it. Jesus said unto her, "Give me to drink." She was surprised that he, being a Jew, should ask water of her, a Samaritan. This very surprise which she expressed led to a most instructive conversation. Read it, and see how plainly Jesus teaches us the nature of true worship. The Jews had their temple at Jerusalem; the Samaritans had theirs on Mount Gerizim. The woman said to Jesus, "Our fathers worshipped in this mountain, and ye say that Jerusalem is the place where men ought to worship." She would ask which was the true place. Jesus declared to her that it was not so much the place, as it was the heart, which made worship what it should be. Read the answer of

Jesus as the New Testament gives it, and then see if the Quaker poet, Barton, has not beautifully expressed it thus:

"Woman, believe me, the hour is near
When He, if ye rightly would hail him,
Will neither be worshipped exclusively here.
Nor yet at the altar of Salem.

For God is a spirit, and they, who aright
Would perform the pure worship he loveth
In the heart's holy temple will seek with delight
That spirit the Father approveth."

Through the knowledge of Christ obtained by the Samaritan woman in this conversation, many of her sect were induced to believe on him.

Shechem, or Sichem, is a very ancient place; though we do not find it mentioned as a city until the time of Jacob, who purchased a piece of land, and dug the well of which we have just spoken. The city lay between the two mountains Ebal and Gerizim. It was made a city of refuge. Joshua 20: 7. 21. 20, 21. Quite a number of events mentioned in the Old Testament occurred here. It was at Shechem Joshua met the assembled people for the last time. It was here that Rehoboam was made king, and the ten tribes rebelled.

In after time Shechem became the chief seat of the people who thenceforth bore the name of Samaritans. They were made up in part of emigrants from other eastern nations. When the Jews returned from their long captivity in Babylon, and began to rebuild Jerusalem and their temple, the Samaritans desired to aid them in their work. "Let us build with you," was their request. The Jews refused to admit them to this privilege; hence a strong hatred between the two sects arose. The Samaritans erected their temple on Mount Gerizim

Shechem received the new name of Neapolis from the Greeks - a name which it retains to the present day. The city has passed through many changes, which, had we time to recount them, might be of deep interest to the reader. But it would take a larger space to do this than we can now occupy. The Samaritans are still here; but their number now is small, not exceeding one hundred and fifty. They have a synagogue, where they preserve several ancient copies of the books of Moses, and among them one ancient manuscript which they believe to be three thousand four hundred and sixty-five years old, saying it was written by Abishua, the son of Phinehas (1 Chron. 6: 3, 4.) The manuscript, so travellers who have seen it say, is very ancient; but they do not all think it so old as the Samaritans pretend it is.

Mount Gerizim is still held in great veneration by the Samaritans. Four times a year they ascend it in solemn procession, to worship. The old feeling of hostility between them and the Jews is still existing.

The city of Neapolis, or, as the Arabs call it, Nablous, is long and narrow, stretching close along the northeast base of Mount Gerizim. The population is about eight thousand souls, all Mohammedans, with the exception of about five hundred Greek Christians, and the one hundred and fifty Samaritans already mentioned. Those who have taken part in its eventful past history are gone. But never shall be heard there a more glorious voice than that which uttered those sublime words of heavenly truth to the woman at Jacob's well.

"ARE WE NOT ALL BROTHERS AND SISTERS?"

BY REV. W.R.G. MELLEN.

That the human race is one, bound together by the strongest and holiest ties, is one of the sublimest truths announced by the Master. Indeed, so close and intimate is the connection subsisting between the various members of the common family, that to tear one from the body would be like following the direction of Solomon to his servant, and dividing the living child in two, leaving life's purple current to spout forth from either half. An appreciation of this truth is what the world, heart-sick and weary as it is, now needs above all things else. And to illustrate and enforce the fact that it is not a vain shadow, but a solid reality, too solemn to be trifled with, and too important to be neglected, - to illustrate this by deeds which bear joy to the joyless and hope to the hopeless, - is *the* work which Christians, the young as well as old, are now called to perform. Will it need the voice of duty, which speaketh as from the skies? This is the great truth, also, which, with all its relations to life and duty, is to be impressed by the present, upon the minds of the rising, generation. This is what my young readers are to learn, - and not simply to learn, but to practise: - that we are all brothers and sisters, no matter in what clime or country we may have been born, or with what complexion we may be clothed.

A little girl, some five years of age, whom the writer of this has often fondled in his arms, had well learned this most important lesson. By pious parents and earnest Sabbath school teachers had she been taught, that to be like Jesus, who took little children in his arms and blessed them, she must love and do good unto all, as brothers and sisters. This had sunk deep into her young and tender mind; and when, on a visit at the house of a friend, she was asked that familiar question, which is so often put to children, - whom she loved, -

After a moment's hesitation she replied, that she loved everybody. "Indeed!" said the querist; "how can that be? You certainly do not love me as well as you do your own brothers and sisters; do you?"

After another short pause she replied, "Yes, I think I do; for *you*, too, are my sister." "*I* your sister?" said the lady, in surprise; "how can that be possible?" Looking up with a countenance in which all heaven's innocence and purity were mirrored, she exclaimed, "Is not God our Father? and are we not all brothers and sisters? and should we not love each other as such?"

There was no further argument to be used. Though hid from many wise and prudent, yet the truth was thus revealed to babes.

Yes, we *are* all brethren and sisters, having a common origin, a common destination, and a common home. And may all those children who read this short article ever recollect this important truth. When you behold a poor, unfortunate man, with torn and filthy garments, and perhaps intoxicated, reeling through the streets, do not hoot after, and throw stones at him, as I have known many boys do, but think within yourselves, "He is our brother."

When one of your number abuses the rest, and you are tempted to injure and beat him, wait till you have said to yourselves, "He is still our brother; and though he has done us wrong, why should we strike or injure him?"

When you see a companion in trouble, and one to whom your assistance can do much good, recollect he is a brother, or she is a sister, and fly to help him. And oh! if all, both old and young, would act upon this principle, how different would be the aspect of affairs from what it now is! Then the kingdom of God would dawn upon us. Then the wolf and the lamb would lie down together, and the lion eat straw like an ox. Then we should be like *little children*, and the blessing-smile of Jehovah would shed upon us choicest benediction.

FORTUNE-TELLING.

A DIALOGUE FOR EXHIBITIONS.

BY JULIA A. FLETCHER.

Sophronia. Come, girls, let us go and have our fortunes told.

Eveline. Oh! I should like it of all things; where shall we go?

Sarah. Let us go to old Kate Merrill's. They say she can read the future as we do the past, by hand, tea-cups, or cards. Come, Mary Ann.

Mary Ann. Excuse me, girls, if I do not go with you. I do not think it is right to have our fortunes told.

Sophronia. Not right? why not?

Mary Ann. Because, if it had been best for us to know the future, I think God would have revealed it to us.

Sarah. Oh, but you know this is only for amusement.

Eveline. Of course, we shall not believe a word she says.

Mary Ann. If it is only for amusement, I think we can find others far more rational and innocent. But depend upon it, girls, you would not wish to go, if there were not in your minds a little of credulous feeling?

Sophronia. Well, I am sure I am not credulous.

Mary Ann. Do not be offended, Sophronia; I only meant that we are all of us more inclined to believe these things than we at first imagine.

Sarah. I think that Mary Ann is right in this respect. I am sure I would not go if I did not think her predictions would come to pass.

Mary Ann. Certainly; I could not suppose you would spend your time and money to hear an old woman tell you things you did not believe.

Eveline. Well, I am sure I do not see any harm in having a little fun once in a while.

Sophronia. No; and I think it is very unkind in Mary Ann to spoil all our pleasures with her whims. She is always preaching to us about giving up our own way for the comfort of others, and I think she ought to give up now, and go with us.

Sarah. Now, really, Sophronia, I think you are the one that is unkind. If Mary Ann is wrong, it is better to convince her of it kindly, and I am sure she will acknowledge it.

Mary Ann. I hope I should be willing to give up a mere whim for the pleasure of those I love so well. But this is not a whim; it is a serious conviction of duty.

Sophronia. Well, I thought you always pretended to be very obliging.

Mary Ann. I have no right to be obliging at the expense of what I deem duty. Our own inclinations we should often sacrifice, our prejudices always, but our sense of duty never.

Eveline. I think, girls, we have done wrong to urge Mary Ann to go, after she had told us her reasons.

Sophronia. Well, then, don't spend any more time in urging her to go, against her will. You know the old proverb "The least said is soonest mended."

Eveline. Well, do not let us go away angry or ill-natured. You asked Mary Ann to say why she thought it was wrong, and we should receive her reasons kindly.

Sarah . So I think; but I wish she would tell us what harm she thinks it would do to go.

Mary Ann. Well, girls, I think, by trying to look into the future, we are apt to grow discontented and restless, and to forget that we have duties to perform in the present. Then, if we do not believe in it, it is a waste of time and money, which might be better employed in relieving the suffering of the poor around us. But the greatest evil of all is, that we should believe even a part; she would of course tell us many little circumstances which would be true of any one; thus we might be led to believe all she said; the prediction would probably work out its own fulfilment, and perhaps render us miserable for life.

Sophronia. Oh, fudge! Mary Ann. This is altogether too bad and ungenerous in you. In the first place, the few cents we give, bestowed as they are on a poor old widow woman, are not wasted, in my opinion, but well spent; - and if I spend an evening, granted to me by my father and mother for recreation, in listening to Old Kate, it is no more wasted than if I spend it with the girls in any other social way. And when you connect fortune-telling and our duties in the present, you make it too serious an affair. *Remember, this is all for sport*.

Mary Ann. It may be so with you, Sophronia; but there are those who seriously believe every word of a fortune-teller, and actually live more in the unseen but expected events of the future, than in faithfully performing their duties in the present. This is true, Sophronia. The contentment and peace of many young minds have been utterly lost, *sold* for the absurd jabbering of old, ignorant, low-bred women, who pretend to read the future. [*In a livelier tone of voice*.] But just say, girls, do you believe there is any connection between tea-leaves and your future lives?

Eveline, Sarah, Sophronia. Why, no!

Mary Ann. Do you believe God has marked the fortunes of thousands of his creatures on the face of cards?

Eveline, Sarah, Sophronia. Certainly not.

Mary Ann. Well, do you believe, if God should intrust the secret events of the future with any of our race, in this age, it would be with those who have neither intellectual, moral, nor religious education - who can be bribed by dollars and cents to say anything?

Sarah, Eveline. No, indeed!

Mary Ann. (Turns to Sophronia,) You do not answer, Sophronia. Let me ask you one or two more questions. Do you suppose Kate Merrill believes that she has a revelation from God?

Sophronia. No, Mary Ann.

Mary Ann. Do you suppose she thinks you believe so?

Sophronia. Why, yes, I do.

Mary Ann. Then, is it benevolent to bestow money to encourage an old woman in telling for truth what she knows to be false?

Sophronia. I doubt whether it is really benevolent.

Mary Ann. And if Old Kate speaks falsely and knows she does so, and you know it, yet spend your time in listening to what she has to say, what good can come of it to head or heart?

Sophronia. None at all, Mary Ann. It is time wasted, and I am convinced that I have been doubly wrong in wishing to go, and in being angry with you. Will you forgive me?

Mary Ann. Certainly, Sophronia. And now, if you wish for amusement, I will be a witch myself, and tell your fortunes for you.

Sophronia. Oh, do tell mine; and be sure you tell it truly. What lines of fate do you see in my hand?

Mary Ann. (Takes her hand and looks at it intently.)

(To Sophronia.)

Passions strong my art doth see.
Thou must rule them, or they rule thee.
If the first, you peace will know;
If the last, woe followeth woe.

Sarah. Now tell mine next.

(To Sarah.)

Too believing, too believing,
Thou hast learned not of deceiving.
Closely scan what seemeth fair,
And of flattering words beware.

Eveline. Now tell me a pleasant fortune, Mary Ann.

(To Eveline.)

Lively and loving, I would not chide thee,
Do thou thy duty, and joy shall betide thee.

Sophronia. Thank you, Mary Ann, for the lessons you have given us. We can now, in turn, tell your fortune, and that is, Always be amiable and sensible as now, and you will always be loved.

THE BOY WHO STOLE THE NAILS.

BY REV. MOSES BALLOU.

I remember well, that, when I was quite a little boy, a circumstance occurred which I shall probably never forget, and which, no doubt, has had some little influence on my life at many different periods since. I will relate it; and I wish all my young readers would remember the story.

My father was somewhat poor. He had no salary for preaching, except for a few months, perhaps not five hundred dollars for forty years of pulpit labor. He maintained his family chiefly from a small farm, and, there being several children, we were deprived of many little things that wealthier parents are accustomed to furnish for theirs. We had few presents, and those chiefly of necessary articles, - school-books, or something of the kind; while toys, playthings, and instruments of amusement, we were left to go without, or take up with such rude and simple ones as we could manufacture for ourselves.

I wanted a small box very much. A handsome little trunk, such as most of my young readers probably have, was too much to hope for, and a plain wooden box, even, I had no means to purchase.

I went without for a long time, and at last determined that I would try to make one. But the materials, - where was I to obtain them? True, my father had pieces of thin boards that would answer, but there were nails, and hinges, and a lock wanting. Where were these to come from?

After trying a variety of methods, I invented a plan for fastening it without a lock, and leather made a very good substitute for hinges, as it was to be out of sight. Still, I wanted nails. There were some old ones about the house, but they were crooked, and broken, and rusty. These would not answer if anything better could be obtained.

My uncle, who at this time lived but a short distance from us, was engaged in building, and I watched the barrel of bright new nails his workmen were using, with a longing eye. O, how I coveted them!

The temptation was too great. I sought the opportunity while the hands were at dinner, and, after cautiously looking about to see that no one was near to observe me, with trembling hands seized upon them, *and stole enough to make my box*. O! how my heart beat as I hurried away across the fields home. I almost expected to see some one start up from every stump and bush on the way, to accuse me of the theft. I hardly dared to look behind me. It seemed as though my old uncle, with frowning brow, was at my very heels. And then, too, the workmen; - were they not suspicious from my hanging about them, and had not some of them watched me? So horrid images began to dance about my brain. Dim visions of court-rooms, and lawyers, and judges, and prisons, and sorrowing parents, and frightened brothers and sisters, rose in awful terror before me. I began to grow dizzy and faint. I had laid up, for a long time, all the pennies I could obtain, which, at that time, amounted to the vast sum of twenty cents, contained in an old-fashioned pistareen; and the hope sprung up in my heart, that, possibly, by paying this to the officers, they would not carry me to jail.

Thought was busy in laying plans for escape, and I reached home in the greatest excitement imaginable.

Well, the deed was now done, and I could not undo it. I was really a thief; and now, as I had got the nails, I thought I might as well use them. I was too anxious about the crime, however, to do this at once. So I hid them away for a week or more, before I ventured to make my box.

Taking such leisure hours as I had, - for I was obliged to work most of the time on the farm, - I crept away in the loft of an old building, and finally succeeded in finishing my task. But, now that the box was done, my troubles were by no means ended. It would be seen. I could not always keep it out of sight. My brothers, and sisters, and playmates, would examine it, and possibly my father would get his eye upon it! Suppose he should, and ask me where those nails came from?

O, how my poor brain was racked to invent some false story by which I could escape detection! I thought of saying that they were old ones which I had polished up so as to appear new, and I even filed down the rust on the head of an old nail to see if they would look sufficiently alike. But nothing of this kind would answer. The cheat, I thought, would be detected; and so I was obliged, after all my trouble and suffering, to keep my box hidden away when it was done. Every time I went to look at it, those bright new nail-heads were staring out at me, ready to reveal my crime to any one who saw them.

For a long time, I did not dare to go to my uncles again. True, he knew nothing of my wrong; but I felt guilty, and did not care to see him. Finally, after some time had passed away, though I had by no means forgotten the theft, and still suffered much every time it was thought of, I ventured to call and see him. I could hardly avoid the impression that he must know what I had done, and would accuse me of it; and when he met me in the yard at his door; patted my cheek with a half-laughing, half-reproving look; asked why I had stayed away from him so long; and said, that, to punish me, he should go and get me some very nice apples from the garden; - I could bear it no longer. It seemed as though my heart would break. What I said, I have now forgotten. I remember that I cried very heartily, and, as soon as my tears would allow it, told him the whole story!

I can still see, fresh in my memory, the sad look that came over him as I confessed my crime; but not a single harsh or unkind word did he utter. He told me that it was very wrong; that I had acted nobly in confessing it; and that, if I had only asked him in the first place, he would gladly have given me all I wanted.

Thinking I had suffered enough already, he promised not to tell my parents, in case I continued a good boy, and advised me to destroy the box and bring him back the nails, as no one could then suspect what had been done but ourselves.

His kindness, I confess, pained me very much. I think nothing could have tempted me to do him any wrong again.

I loved him better than ever before. He never alluded to the subject afterwards, but I always thought of it when I saw him. He died in a short time; and, twenty years after, as I stood by his grave, the circumstance came up, clear and distinct, to my recollection. I have not, indeed, from that to the present hour, felt the least temptation to commit any wrong of the kind without recalling it; and, if all my young readers will think seriously how much suffering that one act cost me, and how much happier I should otherwise have been, I am confident that they will never commit a similar offence so long as they remember the story of *the boy who stole the nails*.

THE CHILDLESS MOTHER.

BY MRS. M.H. ADAMS.

There are many childless mothers in our land. In some homes there never lived a little child to make them happy; but in others the spirits of the little ones have departed. They dwell in another home - the "dear heavenly home." Their mothers, those childless mothers, weep day and night in their loneliness and sadness. This sketch is of a mother who had buried all her little babes - four precious children - all her little family. The mother's name was Ellen Moore.

For many months after the birth of her first child, Ellen was free from sorrow as a bird in the morning. She never thought affliction might come to her blessed home. It was not surprising, for she had never known what bereavement and bitter disappointment were. She was educated to be a child of sunshine. She had always lived amid smiles and tenderness, and when the fearful cloud of sorrow broke, in an unexpected moment, upon her head, she seemed bowed down, never to rise again in health and beauty.

It was a sad day in our neighborhood when Ellen's first little babe died; we all wept. Not so much because he was dead, for we all felt that *he* was at rest; but his dear mother was so sorely troubled, her heart ached so grievously, it seemed as if she too would die. Days and nights Ellen wept, and moaned, and walked her house. The tears seemed to burn their way down her cheeks. She spoke but seldom, yet that pitiful moan she so often breathed out pierced our souls and made us all very sad.

After a few weeks, the consolation we offered her quieted her feelings, and she became calm. She went to church, called on her friends, and attended to her duties at home. But there was ever a sadness in her voice and manners. Her home was so lonely, so strangely still and vacant, and Ellen so silent, that the voice of gladness was not heard in it again until a second beautiful boy was born under its roof.

We were all happy then. Even Ellen smiled as she kissed her dear babe - but a tear followed the smile and the kiss so soon, we knew her wounded heart was not *then* healed. She was very sad, and felt that this babe, too, might only be loaned her for a short time. It was not long before we all felt so. That little face, so pale, so sad, so beautiful, evidently bore the seal of death upon it. He refused all nourishment, and pined slowly away. Ellen knew he must die, but could not say so. She could not shed one tear to relieve her sorrowful heart. She neither spoke nor wept, until her infant was laid in its coffin.

A friend had woven a wreath of beautiful flowers, and laid it on the satin pillow of the coffin, and placed a delicate rose-bud in the little hand of the babe. Ellen went alone to take her last kiss, when, seeing her babe so beautiful in death, she seated herself on the floor and wept freely.

"Who loved my babe so fondly?" said she, when she came from the room. "Who has been so kind and thoughtful of me? It has unsealed my tears; now let me weep alone." We left her. She came out of that room a changed woman. She assisted us in our preparations for the burial of the dead, spoke cheerfully to her husband, conversed freely about her children in heaven, and remarked that henceforth her life should be worthy of a Christian. We buried the sweet babe by the side of his brother, and planted a rose-tree over his grave. Then our thoughts turned to Ellen, whose whole manner indicated resignation and peace.

We were not surprised at the effect of grief upon Ellen, for I have told you she was not educated to bear human misery with much composure. Yet what her parents had left undone seemed to be effected by those severe dispensations of God. Our Father in heaven often educates us by his chastisements, giving us wisdom, patience, hope, trustfulness and resignation, according to the severity with which he afflicts us.

Ellen maintained the same cheerful manner from the time of the burial of her second babe to the birth of her third child. Her friends hoped many blessings for Ellen in the life of this child. It was a daughter, apparently healthy; and as its mother had endured so severe a trial we hoped the Lord would deal mercifully with her in sparing this one to her. For one short year we had reason to hope for the life of the child. But it was too frail a creature for this world, and, like its little brothers, died in early infancy. And its mother - we found her to be a practical Christian indeed.

Instead of moaning and violent grief, she held her babe as it breathed its latest breath, and was first to break the awful silence in the room that succeeded the final struggle, with these words: "She is with her little brothers now, and I have reason to bless the Lord." She could say no more then; and a few large tears fell on the cheek of her babe as it still lay on her lap. Once only did she freely yield to tears. It was when her husband first heard of the death of his babe. His anguish overcame her composure. Soon recovered however, she maintained a truly Christian deportment. The third little grave was opened in the burial lot of Mr. Moore, and the body of this babe laid by its little brothers.

A fourth babe was born in the lonely home of Ellen, and fresh hopes cherished for the long life of her child. The burden of every prayer offered at that family altar was, "Lord, if it be thy will, suffer us to rear this tender child!"

"Yet though I pray thus," said Ellen, "my heart is strong to meet its early death; and if it dies, I shall not mourn as for my first-born. God has afflicted me, but I am profited thereby."

"Very true, Ellen, but if this fourth dear babe is taken from us, we shall almost doubt the mercy of God. How can you, in your present delicate health, endure to lay this last dear babe by the side of the departed ones, and again find your home desolate and silent?"

"My body is weak, Mary, but my spirit is well instructed in resignation, and can calmly bear whatever new affliction God pleases to send. You have called me changed since Alfred died, and sometimes too silent and sad. I am changed and often silent, but not sad. *My* treasures are in heaven, and my communings are more with the spirits of my children in heaven than with the friends who are with me here. And if this child dies, Mary, - if he dies - his death will prepare me for the duties of all the rest of my life."

* * * * *

The beautiful boy passed away just as his little lips had learned to pronounce his mother's name - suddenly, unexpectedly to us all, and all yielded to our grief but Ellen. We greatly feared his father would become insane.

But Ellen - believe me, she was transformed from a child of sunshine to an angel and minister of light in darkness. She sat by her husband as serene and collected as if her babe only slept; not a tear swept her cheek, not a tremulous word fell from her lips, as she soothed her stricken companion; her pale face wore no look of despair, and she directed every funeral preparation with as much composure as if *her* heart had not felt the awful wound. The world called her heartless, - but Christ must have owned her as one of his brightest jewels, almost a perfect disciple. When she spoke, we felt as if some mysterious power from heaven was in our midst. We thought as much of the saint-like fortitude and resignation of our feeble Ellen, and wept as much to witness her calmness and spiritual strength, as for the loss of our interesting little friend.

Our pastor called to offer gospel consolations to the sorrowing mother, but he wept as Ellen greeted him, saying, "God hath much love for us, Brother Ellis, for he chasteneth much. Now, my only prayer is, that Henry may be led to perceive it and be at peace. If you have words of comfort, go to him and still his troubled spirit."

The aged came to console her, but went back to their dwellings feeling that she was as well instructed in the wisdom of heaven as the oldest servant among them. The young and happy came to mingle tears of sympathy with her, but returned to dwell upon her words as upon communications from the spirit-land, rather than from a creature like themselves. Her words found a way to the soul of the most thoughtless, fixing their minds upon heaven, and revealing the unseen glories of a better home, and the beauty of Christian faith in an earthly one.

She was a Christian mother. When she put on Christ, she was "*a new creature*" She believed her first grief was almost a murmuring against heaven. Surely we know she bore an equal love for all her children, but when her last one died, she loved God and her Saviour more, believing fully that God would not do her wrong, - that he only sought the good of his creatures in his dispensations, - that although they seemed grievous and inscrutable to them, he saw the end from the beginning, and chastized whom he loved.

THE MOTHERLESS CHILD.

BY MRS. M.H. ADAMS.

To become a childless mother is indeed one of the most severe afflictions which woman can be called to endure; yet it may be, it is often met with noble, Christian fortitude, with Christian humility and resignation, that soothe the acute pains of the mother's heart, and carry her thoughts away from earth and above its sorrows; so that we feel that she can and has found a balm, and has still left her consolation and happiness. But when we see a little child, whose mother God has taken, as fully realizing its bereavement, its loneliness, its absolute misfortune, as a child can do, we feel that to be a motherless child in this unchristian world, is indeed an affliction for which there seldom appears a balm; though we doubt not our Father hath the balm for this as for every other wound.

A young man sat by the corpse of his faithful wife, the mother of all his little babes. One child was gazing silently and inquiringly at her father, as he held his head weeping and groaning in anguish of spirit. A tender infant of a few weeks lay asleep in the cradle at his side. The young man's mother entered the room, and with tenderness of tone and manner, endeavored to calm his grief; with words of gospel love and faith to comfort him.

"Abby has been to you a kind, faithful and devoted wife, David; an agreeable companion and constant friend. Before God she was a humble child, and before the world a worthy disciple of Christ. You doubtless feel all this, and more. Few can speak evil of her, and very many will sincerely mourn her early death, and sympathize with you in this dreadful hour. But remember, David, you have, before this, professed trust and belief in the promises and love of God. Now is the time to make manifest your Christian faith, your hope in God, your belief in the gospel. Try not to be utterly disconsolate in your loneliness. God is very near to us, although this heavy cloud of sorrow lies between him and us."

They were interrupted by the entrance of the oldest child of the departed one, a sensitive, intelligent boy of six or seven years. Tears were in his eyes as he opened the door, and fell fast into the lap of his father as he tried to speak to him.

"Father," said he, "I have been down in the sitting-room, trying to read my little books; but I think so much of my dear dead mother, I can't read; and the tears come into my eyes so fast, that I can't see the pictures. I went to rock in my little chair, but I saw my mother's empty chair, and my little heart aches very much. It will be very lonesome and sad here, if I don't see mother anywhere. And who will take care of this little baby brother?"

No word was spoken by those present, but their tears and sobs told plainly that they too felt how lonely and sad that home would be without the gentle voice and cheerful song of that "dear mother." As no one checked him, Willie again spoke, and, as well as he could amid sobs and tears, told the bitterness of his young spirit.

"I love you some, father, but not as I did my mother; and now my mother is in heaven, who shall I have to take care of me and kiss me, father; who will say a prayer to me every night? Aunt Susan's prayers are not like mother's; and your voice doesn't sound so sweet by the side of my bed as my mother's did. Oh dear! what did my mother die for, and leave me a poor little motherless boy?"

His father then took him upon his knee, wiped his tears, and soothed him to sleep with gentle caresses. No word could David utter. For a long time he sat with his sleeping boy, beside his dead. The paleness of his cheek, and the frequent sigh, expressed his sorrow. His mother again tried to draw from him an expression of his Christian fidelity, fearing that he was untrue to his God and his Master under a trial so severe. When at length he did speak, a hardened heart might have been moved by his broken sentences and choking words, as he made an effort to assure his anxious parent.

"Mother, I have the utmost confidence in the mercy and goodness of God - even now that he has taken to himself one so very dear. I feel sure there is some great and important lesson which he would have me learn from this sorrowful event. I have all faith that Abby is at rest, and will still love those of us who are left on the earth to mourn. I believe we shall meet each other in the future, that we shall recognize and love each other, with a far more perfect and a purer love than we have cherished here. I shall be lonely, and miss from my hours at home the counsel, the aid, the cheerfulness, sympathy and attentive love of one of the best of women. Her beautiful example in the service of her

Master will often be remembered with deep and sincere grief.

"All this I could bear calmly; if it were more bitter, I could bear it and not weep. But to think of my children - as motherless babes; to hear Willie tell his sorrow, and mourn so bitterly in his tender years for a mother - so dear; to feel that with his susceptibility and keen sensitiveness he realizes so fully his loss; to hear him sob on his pillow at night, and, when alone, call himself 'little motherless Willie;' - oh, mother! what man or Christian would not bow beneath a burden like this? - It is the contemplation of *four motherless children* that wounds me most. It seems to me Abby herself would not reprove me, could those cold lips now bring me a message from her spirit in heaven."

* * * * *

With expressions like those in the chamber of the dead was every hour in the home of David embittered, for weeks and months, by the little mourning child. He gathered flowers and laid them before his father, saying, "I don't suppose you care about them, father; but my mother isn't here to take them. I pick them because they look up into my face as if mother was somewhere near them. But they wither on my hand, and hold down their heads, just as I want to do now my mother is dead."

Every object at home seemed to remind Willie of his mother, and keep his bereavement uppermost in his thoughts. He did not weep as much after a few weeks, but through all his boyhood there rested a sadness on his countenance, that indicated a mournful recollection of that dear mother. Through his whole life he felt that he was like a tender branch lopped from the parent-tree; like a lamb sent out from the fold while too young to meet the storms and travel the dangerous paths of which he often heard from his mother. This idea seemed ever present, and served many times to hold him back from adventurous pursuits and untried schemes. "I don't know - but I should have known had my dear mother lived," was the expression of his general course in life.

As long as he was a child he spoke often and tenderly of his mother. He cherished a remembrance of her faithful admonitions and precepts, as vivid as might have been expected from a child bereaved at the age of eight or ten. When older, he realized more fully his loss, especially when he met one whom he believed to be *a good mother*. He then seldom spoke of his mother; but his visits to the grave-yard, his sadness on the anniversary of the day of her death, his conversations about her with his brothers and sister, the value he attached to every token of her love to him, convinced us that he remembered her with deep affection.

When a young man, he was several times beguiled by the tempter into forbidden paths, and his eyes were not opened to behold the danger until the fangs of the serpent pierced deeply into his heart. Then most fully did he realize that he was *poor motherless William*; that he was abroad in the world without those most effectual safeguards against sin, a good mother's counsels and a mother's daily prayers; that while others could express unreservedly to their mothers their hopes or fears, their success or misfortune, their faithfulness in thc hour of temptation or weakness under its power, and be counselled, encouraged, urged or entreated anew, - he could only go to his mother's grave and shed bitter tears of repentance in loneliness, or withdraw himself from all around him, and, *a poor motherless child,* call up the dim remembrance of that young and cheerful being who once called him her precious son, her treasured child, - and weep the more bitterly that no answering voice or smile, or look of encouragement or hope, met *him* in this sinful world!

Oh ye who have hearts to feel, who profess Christian principles to guide you, and the holy love of our Master for your example, seek out the *motherless child* of the poor, the ignorant, the vicious, and by the power of Christ which is within you, according to the measure of that power, strive to be like fond mothers to the thousands who cry "We have no dear mother - our mother is in heaven - is dead - and we know not what is right or what is wrong!" Help and pity them. Rescue them from that heart-breaking loneliness and sorrow that prey incessantly on the feelings of a sensitive, intelligent, *motherless child.*

FAITH.

BY MRS. E.R.B. WALDO.

Upon the peaceful breast of Faith
My troubled soul hath found repose,
Free from the sad and starless gloom
That doubting scepticism knows.

Though disappointment, care, and pain,
Have bent my heart to their decree,
One thought hath ever led me on,
It is, *that it was so to be*.

Oft would my weary spirit faint,
My heart yield almost to despair,
Did not "a still small voice" exclaim,
"There is no change, but God is there."

That mighty power which points the shaft,
And forms the spirit to endure,
Will, in its own peculiar way
And time, perform the wondrous cure.

Still may my soul, through faith, rely
Upon the promises of God;
His mercy see in every change,
And learn to bless his chastening rod.

THE SNOW-BIRDS. A DIALOGUE.

BY MRS. C. HIGHBORN.

Clarissa. Pray, Mary, what are you going to do with those crumbs which you hold in your hand?

Mary. I am going to feed my snow-birds with them; and I should be very happy to have you go with me. I know you will enjoy seeing how merrily they hop about and flutter their wings, and seem to chirp out their thanks as they pick up the food I throw them.

C. Thank you for your invitation; but I beg you will excuse me; it may be pretty sport for you, but, for my part, I can enjoy myself much better to stay here and arrange my baby-things, for I expect some girls to see me this afternoon. I cannot conceive what there is in those ugly-looking snow-birds to interest you; they are not handsome, surely; they have not a single bright feather; and, as for their songs, they sound like the squeak of a sick chicken.

M. I am sorry to hear you speak so of my favorites; for, though they are not so brilliant in their colors as many that flutter around us in the summer, yet to me they tire dearer than any others, and far more beautiful than those of a gaudier hue.

C. Well, you have a queer taste, I must confess; you remind me of the philosopher I read of in the story-book, who thought a toad the most beautiful of God's creatures. Come, perhaps you can show me why they are entitled to your regard, and point out their beauties.

M. I will cheerfully comply with your request, for nothing gives me more pleasure than to speak of the good qualities of my friends. Examine them for a moment and see how exquisitely they are formed, and, though not gaudy in their colors, yet their feathers are soft and glossy. But these are trifles comparatively; what most endears them to me is their constancy.

C. That is a new idea, indeed. Constancy in snow-birds! Please explain yourself, Mary.

M. Well, they seem to me like those rare friends that love us best in adversity, when the bright summer of prosperity, with its attendant joys, has fled, and the winter of sorrow and misfortune shuts out, with its dark clouds, the light of life, and withers, with its frosts, the few flowers which bloom along its pathway. There are summer friends, Clara, as well as summer birds, and they both wear brilliant colors, and sing enchanting songs, but they depart with the sunshine; the first leave us to battle the storms of adversity, and the others, the cold and barren prospect of winter; these little snow-birds, however, remain, and through all its dark hours they cheer us by their presence. They seem to tell us that we are not entirely destitute of pleasure, but that the darkest hours have something of beauty; and, while they serve to awaken in our minds a remembrance of the bright days that have gone, they bid us look forward to the end of our sorrows, and welcome the bright spring days, which shall return to us the joys that departed.

C. I declare! you have preached quite a sermon, and from a funny text; I confess there is both truth and poetry in what you say. I do not wonder that you love the snow-birds, if they awaken such pleasant and pretty thoughts in your mind. Henceforth I will love them myself, for the good lesson that, through you, they have imparted. I trust you will forgive me the rudeness of laughing at you.

M. Cheerfully, Clara; but learn from this never to despise any of God's creatures; they can all teach us some important and beautiful lesson which we should be happy to heed. And now, if you please, we will go and feed the snow-birds.

C. With all my heart!

MOUNT CARMEL.

SELECTED.

Mount Carmel is a high promontory, forming the termination of a range of hills running northwest from the plain of Esdraelon. Mount Carmel is the southern boundary of the Bay of Acre, on Acca, as it is called by the Turks; its height is about fifteen hundred feet, and at its foot, north, runs the brook Kishon, and a little further north the river Belus.

Mount Carmel is celebrated in Scripture history as the place where Elijah went up when he told his servant to look forth to the sea yet seven times, and the seventh time he saw a little cloud coming up from the sea "like a man's hand," when the prophet knew that the promised rain was at hand, and girded up his loins, and ran before Ahab's chariot even to the gates of Jezreel. (1 Kings xviii. 44-46.)

Towards the sea is a cave, where it has been supposed that Elijah desired Ahab to bring Baal's false prophets, and where fire from heaven descended on the altar he erected. The present appearance of Carmel is thus described by Dr. Hogg, who visited it in 1833. "The convent on Mount Carmel was destroyed by the Turks in the early part of the Greek revolution. Abdallah, the Turkish pasha, who commanded the district in which

Carmel is situated, not only razed their convent to the ground, but blew up the foundations, and carried the materials to Acre for his own use. The convent is now being rebuilt, or probably is now completely finished, the funds having been supplied by subscriptions solicited all over Europe, and a great part of the East, by one of the brethren, Giovanni Battista, who has travelled far and wide for that purpose." Dr. Hogg gives the following account of the condition of the place at the time of his visit.

"The whole fabric is of stone, and, when completed, will possess the solidity of a fortress. The first story only is at present finished, and hereafter will be solely appropriated to the accommodation of travellers, when another, to be raised above, will be exclusively devoted to permanent inmates. In the centre a spacious church has been commenced, and already promises to be a fine building. The principal altar will be placed over the cave so long held sacred as the retreat of the prophet. This natural cavern exhibits at its farther extremity some signs of having been enlarged by art. When the edifice above is complete, it will be converted into a chapel; and a projecting ledge of rock, believed to have been the sleeping-place of the prophet, will then be the altar. The superior himself kindly conducted me to see one of the celebrated caves which everywhere abound in the district of Mount Carmel. Descending two thirds of the mountain by a narrow path, scooped in the rock, we entered an enclosure of fig-trees and vines, where several caverns, that of old belonged to the Carmelites, are now inhabited by a Mohammedan saint and his numerous progeny. We first entered a lofty excavation of beautiful proportions, at least fifty feet long, with a large recess on one side, - every part chiselled with the nicest care, and inscribed with numerous Greek initials, names, and sentences. Here Elijah is believed to have taught his disciples, and hence its name, 'the school of the prophets.' Some smaller adjoining caverns, fronted with masonry, now form the residence of the saint and his family. A deep cistern for the preservation of water has been hewn in the rock, and the entrance is closed by a gate shaded inside by vines.

"The memory of Elijah is equally venerated by Christians and Moslems; and the votaries of each faith are liberally allowed access to the several caves. At the time of our visit the general appearance of Mount Carmel was dry and sterile; but the superior assured us that in spring it was clothed in verdure and beauty."

THE PHILOSOPHY OF LIFE.

BY MISS ELIZABETH DOTEN

"Daily striving, though so lonely,
Every day reward shall give,
Thou shalt find by striving only,
And in loving, thou canst live."
Miss Edwards.

"On dear!" said Annie Burton, as she sat down under the old apple-tree by the spring; "I wonder what ails me; there's been such a choking feeling in my throat all this afternoon, and though I winked and swallowed with all my might, the tears would come in spite of myself. Here I've been wandering for more than three hours, up hill and down, through brambles and brier-bushes; my hands are scratched and bloody, and the sun has burnt me as brown as a berry. Three long precious hours in the sunny month of August! and what does it all amount to? Why, I have picked a basket of berries that can be eaten in half an hour; and here is a bunch of flowers for little Katie, that she will take and admire, and then tear to pieces; that will be the end of them. But that isn't the worst of all; no, not by a great deal; there is a great rent in my frock, gaping and staring at me, waiting to be mended; and nobody knows how long 't will take me to do that. Oh dear!

how I hate to work! I don't see how it is; there's mother takes care of the children, sews, makes bread and washes the dishes, just as willingly and cheerfully as if she were playing on the piano or reading a pleasant book. They say that good people are always happy; but I *never* am. Oh, I believe I am the worst creature that ever lived!" and she bent her head upon her lap and burst into tears.

It was not long before she was roused by the sound of footsteps; she raised her head, and saw an old woman coming down the road with a large basket on her arm. She looked tired and weary, as well she might be, for she had travelled a long distance; it was a hot, sultry afternoon, and every footstep stirred a cloud of dust. She came towards the spring; but before she reached it, she struck her foot against a stone and fell.

"Have you hurt you?" exclaimed Annie, as she sprung to her side.

"Not a bit, not a bit," she replied, as she shook the dust from her apron, and replaced the things that had fallen from her basket.

"Oh, yes, you have!" said Annie; "see, the blood is streaming down your arm!"

"Oh that's nothing; only a scratch. Blessings on the good Father that watches over me! I might have broken my arm, and that would have been a deal worse! How fortunate I happened to fall just by the spring here! I've been longing for a drink of cold water, and I sha'n't need it any the less for getting such a mouthful of this hot dust."

"Heart's dearest!" she exclaimed, as she put down the iron dipper that always hung by the spring, after having satisfied her thirst, "what is it troubles you? Such sorrowful eyes and a tearful face belong only to older heads and more sinful hearts; and God forbid it even to them, unless it is wrung out of the agony of their very souls; for though his providences are just and wise, yet nature must have its way sometimes."

"Oh," she replied, as the tears filled her eyes again, "I have been crying to think how wicked I am."

"Well-a-day!" said the old woman, looking rather droll; "it's very strange such a young creature as you should come down here to weep on account of great wickedness. You don't look much like a Salem witch, or a runaway from the house of correction."

Annie could not help laughing at such an idea; but as the smile passed away, the troubled waters of her heart seemed to burst forth in a flood, and she wept violently.

"Ah," said the old woman, shaking her head sorrowfully: "I ought not to have spoken thus; I see how it is. Poor lamb! she hears the voice of the Shepherd calling her, but she is bewildered and knows not the way to the fold; and may the Lord Jesus look upon me, as he did upon his sinful servant Peter when he denied him, if I fail to point out to this dear child the path wherein he himself has taught me to tread."

She sat down beside Annie and laid her arm gently around her. "There's a dear girl," said she, raising her head, and putting back the locks of moist hair; "listen to me a little while, and I will tell you what will make you happier." She took the cool waters of the spring, and bathed her burning forehead, and washed away all traces of dust and tears. The water had a cooling and soothing effect upon Annie's troubled brain.

"There now," said the good dame; "don't you feel better?"

"Yes," said Annie, almost cheerfully.

"Well," she continued, "God's love is just like this spring; it is full and free to all. Now don't you suppose, if you could cleanse and purify your heart from all traces of sin and sorrow in its blessed waters, just as you bathe your face in this spring, that you would feel happier and better."

"Yes," said Annie, slowly and thoughtfully, as if a new idea was passing through her mind.

"Well then, I will tell you how. I have felt just as you do now. When I was a girl I was a restless, idle creature; useless to others, and a burden to myself. Of course I was unhappy, miserable. It was in vain that I went to school with such a discontented mind. I had a harder lesson to learn than any that my teacher could learn me. God grant you may not have to learn it in the same way that I did! I learned it by experience; a sorrowful way that is to learn anything, although it is slow and sure; you may be pretty certain that you never will forget it. I have found out, by experience, that the only way that we can live and be happy, is by loving and serving others, just as the blessed Jesus did; and if you will try it you will find it so."

"Oh," said Annie, "I am a little girl. What good can I

do? If I was the Lord Jesus, I would go about doing good; then I would cast out devils, and heal the sick, and raise the dead."

"Yes, yes; I know you are yet but a 'wee thing,' and have much to learn; but 'the race is not always to the swift and the battle to the strong;' it isn't the tallest men and the oldest heads that do the most good in the world. But I'll tell you what *you can* do, if you can't work miracles; though there's many a devil cast out in these days of sin and sorrow, that men know not of; those who struggle and strive with the Evil One, and thrust him out of the doors of their heart, do not sound a trumpet before them in the streets, for they are true followers of the dear Lamb of God. That same old spirit of selfishness that tempted Eve in the garden of Eden has gone through the world like a creeping, wily serpent ever since. It has wound itself round and round our hearts, coil upon coil, until we scarce seem to have any heart at all. It is this that troubles you, and you must cast it out; you must forget your own interest, and learn everybody to love you; then you can't help loving everybody, and you will be happy. Oh, it will be hard, very hard, to do this; you will stop, and perhaps turn back; but when it is the darkest you must take the gentle hand that our dear brother, the Lord Jesus, stretches out to you, and he will lead you safely to the very bosom of the Father.

"But look up, dear one, the sun has gone down behind the hill, and you must hasten homeward. The mother bird must needs feel anxious when her nestlings are away. But don't forget what I have told you."

"No," said Annie, raising her head, for she had been thinking earnestly; every word that her kind friend had spoken went with a powerful influence to her heart; "I will *try* and *do what I can,"* said she.

"Ay," said the old woman, "that's right! not even an angel can do more. But stop," she added; "do you remember what day it is?"

"Yes," said Annie.

"Well then, just a year from this time, if the Lord permits, we will meet again by this spring. Now good night, and may the blessing of the Great Father go with you."

"Good night," said Annie, and with a cheerful heart and light footstep, she hastened homeward.

No sooner did she come in sight of her home, than she perceived a horse and carriage standing by the gate. She recognized it in a moment; it was the doctor's. A cold shudder passed over her, and an indefinable fear entered her mind. She hastened onward and entered the house.

Upon the bed lay little Katie; her eyes fixed upon the wall, seemingly unconscious of all that passed around her, sending forth low moans, as if in great pain. Beside her sat the doctor, counting the beatings of her pulse, and closely observing the alterations of her countenance.

"I cannot give you much encouragement," said he. "It is a disease of the brain. All shall be done for her that is possible, but I fear there is not much hope."

Alas! it was even so; all was done in vain. She laid day

after day, a helpless sufferer. It was long before the vital energy was spent; but through all this weary time, there was one constant watcher by her bed-side.

Annie, with the impression of a deep truth upon her soul, felt that *now* was the time to act, and most faithfully did she perform her duty. And when, at last, sweet Katie died, with a warm gush of tears she laid one of the flowers that she had gathered from the hill-side upon her bosom, and clasping her arms around her mother's neck, she said: "Mother, dear sister is gone, and now I must be both Annie and Katie to you; and if God will help me, I shall be more of a blessing to you than I ever yet have been."

Oh, it was like a ray of sunshine to that weeping mother's heart, to hear her once wayward child speak thus! and though it was like taking away the life-drops from her heart to give up her cherished little one, yet she felt there was still a great blessing remaining for her.

Time passed on. Autumn came with its ripened fruits and golden foliage; winter laid his glittering mantle upon the streams and hill-tops, and spring brought blossoms for little Katie's grave.

Annie, the gentle Annie, where was she?

Firm to her purpose, she had gone onward. At times the struggle was hard indeed. Then she would go to the spring, and kneel down, and talk with her Good Father, until the evil feelings had left her heart, and the cheerful smile came again to her countenance.

At length summer, bright, beautiful summer, beamed

over the land once more, and as it drew to a close it brought the day on which Annie was to meet her friend at the spring.

It was the close of the Sabbath, and the last rays of the setting sun streamed through the branches of the trees that surrounded the spring, and tinged its waters with a rosy light. There sat the old lady, looking anxiously up the road.

"I wonder why she don't come," said she. "Perhaps the young thing has forgotten me. Sure 'twould be a sorrow to me if I thought she had."

"No indeed," said a pleasant voice. A light form sprang from a clump of bushes close by, and she felt a warm kiss upon her cheek. "No, I have not forgotten you, but I have come to tell you how happy I am. Oh, I have seen trouble and sorrow *enough*, since I saw you; but for all that, I am much happier than I was then. You told me that I must learn to love everybody, and so I did; and now it seems as if everybody and everything loved me, even our old cat and dog. Strange, isn't it?"

"Heart's dearest!" said the old woman, as soon as she could speak, wiping away the tears from her eyes with the corner of her apron; "there's a philosophy in all things, even in baking bread and washing dishes; but the true philosophy of life consists in loving and doing; and, blessed be God! that is so plain, that the least of his children can understand it."

THE STARVING POOR OF IRELAND.

BY REV. J.G. ADAMS.

A wail comes o'er the ocean,
Though faint, yet deep with woe!
A nation's poor are falling
Before the direst foe!
Grim Famine there hath seized them,
And over Erin's land
The multitudes are perishing
Beneath his blasting hand!

The father gives his morsel
To his imploring child,
Himself imploring mercy, too,
With voice and visage wild.
The ever-faithful mother
Her portion, too, will share
With those who lean upon her,
And plead her dying care.

Then father, mother, children,
Must listen, one and all,
To Famine's surer, sterner voice -
To Death's relentless call.
For means are all exhausted;
Bread! bread! There is no more!
And in that once glad cabin

The conflict now is o'er.

Fond, faithful hearts there perished;
Affections deep and true
As other homes and loved ones
Now know, or ever knew.
And why this visitation
So sweeping and so sore?
Why? why? Repeat the question
The wide world o'er and o'er!

In that same land is plenty,
Profusion, wealth, and power,
Enough to stay the famine-plague
This very day and hour.
Yes, while the poor are starving
By scores and hundreds even,
Riches and luxury send up
Their impious laugh to heaven!

Wrong! wrong! this destitution,
While there are means to save
A nation of strong-hearted men
From famine and the grave.
Thanks, thanks for riches! but a woe
To this our earth they bring,
So long as they shall fail to save
God's poor from suffering!

THE SABBATH SCHOOL FESTIVAL.

BY REV. HENRY BACON.

In these days of "exhibitions" and "excursions" which give such rich pleasure to our Sabbath school children, it may be well to turn back something over twenty years, and see what used to be "great things" to the pupils of the Sunday schools. The only festival I ever knew while in a Sabbath school, in my youth, was at Dr. Baldwin's church, Boston. As I was cradled in a different faith, I ought to tell how I came to be a scholar in a Baptist school; and I will do so, as it may give a good hint to some teachers to be impartial.

At the school I attended a decision was made to give a silver medal to the best scholar. A good many of us worked hard for it, especially the boys in the round pews near the pulpit, who had reason to think that the prize would fall to one of their number. A right good feeling prevailed amongst them; all were willing to acquiesce in whatever should be the decision of the superintendent or committee. When the time for decision came, a lad, the son of a deacon, and who had left school and had not been at school for six months, was sent for, and *to him* the silver medal was given! We all felt outraged, but did not dare to say much. I begged my parents, with good reasoning, to let me go to another school, where I had many friends; and I went to Dr. Winchell's, in Salem street, where Mr. John Gear was superintendent.

What lessons I did get! Whole chapters were recited from the New Testament, because so many verses brought me a reward, so many rewards a mark, and so many marks *a book*! We had no libraries then. Well, the annual meeting came round, and one evening the school met and marched down to Dr. Baldwin's church. I remember the children did the singing, and while they were singing, of course, I sung; and I have not forgotten how crest-fallen I felt when Mr. Gear came along, and whispered to me, "Don't sing *so loud*;" but he might just as well have said, "Don't sing," because I knew he did not want me to sing, for I could not keep time. But it was festival-night, and he was extremely good-natured, and did not wish to cut short the privileges of any. A prayer was offered, and then we sung again. A big man, in a large black silk gown, got up, and delivered a sermon; but we did not heed it as we ought to have done, because some *tea-chests* were ranged along at the base of the pulpit. It was not the *tea-chests* that attracted our attention, but the sweets that we knew were *in* them.

After the sermon was over, and the scholars were ranged in order, in single file, they marched up to the table near the chests, and each one received *a quarter of a sheet of gingerbread!* How rich we were! How sweet the cake tasted! We were in perfect ecstasies at the "great piece" given to each of us! Such rows of happy children are seldom seen, and all because two cents worth of gingerbread was given to them all alike! We had thought of it for weeks, and it was delightful to anticipate the occasion. We felt paid for all the trouble we had met in learning lessons, in getting to school on rainy days, and keeping still and orderly when we got there. And why all this happiness from so slight a cause? Because we all felt loving and happy; we loved our teachers and our school; and it seemed *so odd* to get gingerbread in the church and from the Sabbath school superintendent.

But how is it now? A long ride or sail; swings, music, cakes, pies, fruit, lemonade, and a vast variety of "good things," must be had, or else the Sabbath school children do not have "a good time!" After all this is had and enjoyed, I do not believe it is any better than our simple quarter of a sheet of gingerbread, unless the scholars love each other more, and their schools better, than we did. Do *you*, reader?

NELLY GREY.

"Nelly! Nelly! Where can the child be? Nelly! Nelly!" But Nelly Grey was away off in dreamland, and the cheerful tones of her mother's voice fell all unheeded upon her ear, as did the impatient touch of her little dog Frisk's cold nose upon her hand. She was sitting on the last step of the vine-covered portico in front of the cottage, - the warm June sun smiling down lovingly upon her, and the soft wind kissing the little rings of chestnut-colored hair that clustered about her temples.

What could make the child so quiet? It must be some weighty matter that would still *her* joyous laugh. Why, she was the merriest little body that ever hunted for violets. There was a laugh lodged in every dimple of her sunny face, and her busy little tongue was all the day long carolling some happy ditty.

"Nelly, what are you dreaming about? I've been calling you this long time, and here you are in this warm sun, almost asleep."

"No, no! mother dear, I've only been thinking, and haven't heard you call once. Only to think that you couldn't find me mother! how funny!"

"And what has my little girl been thinking of?" said

Mrs. Grey, as she lifted Nelly into her lap, and smoothed hack the silky curls from her brow. Nelly laid her rosy cheek close to her mother's, and wound her small arms about her neck, and told her simple thoughts in a low, sweet voice.

"You know it's strawberry time, mother, don't you?"

"Yes, darling."

"Well, I was thinking, if you would let me, I could pick a big basket full, they are so thick over in our meadow; and maybe Mrs. Preston would buy them of me, for she gives Mr. Jones a heap of money every year for them."

"And what does Nelly want of a heap of money?"

"Why, mother, little Frisk wants a brass collar, - don't you, Frisk?" Frisk barked and played all sorts of antics to show his young mistress he was very much in need of one. "Think how pretty it would be, mother, round Frisk's glossy neck. Oh, say that I may - do, do, mother!"

Nelly's pleading proved irresistible, and her mother tied her little sunbonnet under her chin, gave the "big basket" into her hands, and the little girl trudged merrily off, with Frisk jumping and barking by her side to see his young mistress so happy.

Shall I tell how the long summer afternoon wore away, dear little reader, and how the big basket was filled to the tip-top and covered with wild flowers and oak leaves? Shall I tell, or shall I leave you to guess, my little bright eyes? You say, yes? Well, I will tell you about her walk to Mrs. Preston's after the sun had gone down and the azure blue sky had become changed to a soft, golden hue.

It was a pleasant walk under the drooping trees, and Nelly Grey, swinging her basket carefully on her arm, tripped lightly on her way. Oh, how her blue eyes danced with joy as she looked down upon the little merry Frisk trotting by her side; her bright lips parted as she murmured, "Yes, yes, Frisk shall have a nice new collar, with 'Nelly Grey's dog, Frisk,' written upon it;" then Frisk played all sorts of funny antics again, probably by way of thanks.

Ah! but what calls that sudden blush and smile to Nelly's face? - and she had well nigh stumbled, too, and spilt all her strawberries. No wonder she started, for, emerging from under the shadow of the trees, was a handsome lad some half a head taller than Nelly. He was gazing, too, with a witching smile into her face, waiting till it should be the little maiden's pleasure to notice him. She nodded her pretty little head as demurely as a city belle, laid her small hand lovingly upon Frisk's curly coat, and walked with a slower and less bounding step than before. But Phil Morton was not to be abashed at this; so he stepped lightly up to Nelly, saying,

"Let me carry your basket; it is too heavy for you."

The little girl, with many injunctions to be careful and not tip it over, delivered the basket to him; she then told him her project of buying Frisk a collar with the money got by the selling of the strawberries, which young Phil approved of very much, and offered to go with her to buy it, for he knew somebody, he said, that kept them for sale. Nelly joyfully assented to his offer, and thanked him heartily, too, for his kindness.

"There, Phil, we are almost there. I can see the long study window; we have only to pass the widow Mason's cottage, up the green lane, and we shall be there."

On they walked, laughing merrily for very lightness of heart, till they were close beside the poor widow's low cottage window. Suddenly Nelly stopped, and the laugh was hushed upon her bright lips. "Did you hear it, Phil?" she said softly. "Hear what, Nell?" and Phil turned his black eyes slowly round, as if he expected to see some fairy issue from the grove of trees near by. "Why, Lucy Mason's cough. Mother says she will not live to see the little snow-birds come again. Poor, dear Lucy!" The great tear-drops rolled fast over Nelly's red cheeks, and fell like rain upon her little hand. "Oh, Phil, I'll tell you what; - I'll give these strawberries to Lucy. She used to love them dearly."

"Poh! poh! Nelly; what a silly girl! to give them away when Mrs. Preston will give you such a deal of money for them!"

"But, Phil, Lucy's mother is poor; she can't buy them for her, and you can't think how well Lucy loves them."

"Well, what if she does, and what if she is poor? can't her mother pick them over in the fields, if she wants them so bad? I wouldn't give them away."

"For shame, Phil Morton! To think of poor old Mrs. Mason's going over in the fields to pick strawberries, leaving Lucy all alone, and so sick! I shouldn't have thought it of you, Phil. No, indeed I shouldn't. Give me the basket," said Nelly sorrowfully; "I shall give them to Lucy." Phil silently handed the basket to her, and, without speaking, he followed Nelly as she went round to the cottage door.

The tears ran silently down the poor widow's cheek as she led the children to her sick child's room, for it touched her heart to see young and thoughtless children so attentive to her poor Lucy. "And did you come all this way, you and Phil, Nelly, to bring me these nice strawberries?" without waiting for her to reply, she turned to a little choice tea-rose that stood beside her, and, breaking off two half-blown buds, she gave them to Phil and Nelly, saying as she did so, "It's all I have to give you, darlings, for your kindness to me, but I know that you will like them as coming from your sick friend."

The bright blood flashed over Phil's dark brow and crimsoned even his ears. Poor Phil! The shame and remorse of those few minutes washed away his unthinking sin, and Nelly forgave him, and tried with all her power to make him forget it. But the kind though thoughtless boy was not satisfied until he had sent Lucy a pretty little basket filled with rare and beautiful flowers, gathered from his father's large garden. Then, and not till then, did he look with pleasure upon the rose Lucy had given him.

Some time after the above occurrence, perhaps a week, Nelly was sitting in her low rocking-chair, under the shadow of the portico, sewing as busily as her nimble little fingers would let her, when a shadow darkened the sunlit walk leading to the house. Nelly saw it, and knew well enough who it was; but there she sat, her pretty little mouth pursed up, and her merry blue eyes almost closed, working faster than ever.

"Oh! is it you, Phil?" she exclaimed, as Phil Morton bounded lightly over the railing beside her, (for he disdained the sober process of walking up the steps;) "how you frightened me!" *He* frighten *her!* Though he was naughty sometimes, and scared the little birds, he would not think of frightening Nelly Grey. No, not he.

"Oh! Phil, I have something to show you," said the little girl, after a while, and then she raised her voice and called, "Frisk! Frisk!" Frisk was not far away from Nelly, and presently he came lazily along, shaking his silky coat as if he did not quite relish being waked from his nap so abruptly.

"But what is that shining so brightly around his neck - can it be a collar? Well, it is, sure enough. But where *did* you get it, Nell?" said Phil, turning to her in amazement.

"Mrs. Preston, the minister's wife, gave it to me; how she came to know I wanted it, I can't think."

"But I can, Nell. She heard us when we were talking, I'll bet; for you know she came in just after we did, and she gave it to you for being so good."

"Oh no, Phil! I only did what anybody else would have done."

"*Anybody*? You know *I* didn't want to Nelly," said Phil sadly.

"Oh, never mind *that*, Phil; you did afterward, you know."

"Well, but, Nell, I *know* she gave it to you for being so good. Isn't there something on the collar?"

"No, only Frisk's name;" and she turned to examine it with Phil.

"There, Nell! what do you call this?" and Phil triumphantly held up the edge of the collar, on which was written, "*Nelly's reward for self-denial.*"

"Why, Phil, I never saw it before; isn't it queer?"

"Queer, that you didn't *see* it before? Yes; but it isn't queer that she gave it to you No, not at all; I should have thought she would."

"Oh, Phil, how you praise me! you mustn't," said Nelly, her pink cheeks deepening into scarlet.

She deserved praise, did not she? for she was a very good little girl. But I will not tire you with any more about her now. So good-by, my sweet little reader.

NORA.

THE FOUR EVANGELISTS.

BY REV. H.R. NYE.

My Young Friends:

I love to hear and to tell stories nearly as well as when I was a child; but I cannot write them for others to read. Even *small* children are sometimes *great* critics. At any rate, I shall not venture at story-telling here.

You have all read some portions of the book we call the Bible. But do you know who wrote the Bible? at what time it was written? or anything of the men by whom it was composed? It was not written by any one man, at one time, and by him sent out to all men in every part of the world; but by various persons, in different ages, and first addressed to particular churches or people. I will not attempt, in this article, to furnish you with an account of all the individuals, Moses, David, Isaiah, Paul, John, and others, who wrote portions of the sacred volume; but I will try to give you some sketches of *the four Evangelists,* Matthew, Mark, Luke, and John, who wrote the four *gospels*, or Lives of Jesus, to which their names are now attached. And,

1st, of MATTHEW, by whom the *first* gospel was composed. He was called, also, Levi. He was a Jew, born in the province of Galilee. We suppose that from his youth he was familiar with the worship of the synagogue and temple, and educated strictly in the religion of Moses. He filled the office of a publican, was a collector of taxes from the Jews, to which place he was appointed by the Romans, who, in his day, ruled over Judea. While engaged in these duties, he became acquainted with the preaching, miracles, and character of Jesus, the despised Nazarene, and left all, - his business, friends, home, - to follow him. He journeyed with Jesus in his ministry, and, after his Master went up to heaven, he left his own land to preach the gospel among the Gentiles. Some people suppose that he was a martyr, but this is not well established. Matthew wrote his gospel either in Hebrew or Greek, (some say both,) about 1800 years since, - very soon after his Master had finished the labors of his mission, and returned unto his Father. I said, I think, that this man left all; made many sacrifices to become Jesus' disciple. But we do not find this in *his* book. With other virtues, he was an *humble* man, quite too modest to praise himself. Luke, in his narrative, mentions this fact concerning Matthew. Modesty is a rare virtue; an ornament to the aged, and very beautiful in the young. But I will tell you,

2d, of Mark, sometimes called John, and once, John Mark, in the New Testament. Very little is known concerning this man. He was probably born in Judea, and, it is supposed, was converted to Christianity by the preaching of the ardent, zealous Peter. At one time, he was the companion of Paul and Barnabas; but, when a quarrel sprang up between these men, each went his way. Christians quarrelled then sometimes as well, or as bad, as in our days. Chiefly, Mark travelled with Peter, as he went forth among Jews and Gentiles, and aided him in his arduous toils. He went, at last, to Egypt, where he planted churches, and where, also, he died. Mark was not an apostle; neither did he attend on the ministry of Jesus. Do you ask, how, then, could he write a correct account of our Saviour's life? Here is one fact worth remembering. Mark was the companion of Peter, who was an apostle, who saw the miracles and heard the discourses of Christ. He examined the account which Mark had written, and gave it his approval, as being correct, - true. Very few men who write histories have vouchers like his. So, did we not regard the Bible-writers as inspired men, we should place the utmost confidence in the truth of Mark's gospel. He composed it about A.D. 65. We come now,

3d, to LUKE. He was a Gentile, - all people not born in Judea were called Gentiles, - born in Antioch, the capital of Syria, where the disciples of Jesus first were called Christians. Luke was a learned man, we are told, having studied in the famous schools of his own land, also of Greece and Egypt. He was a physician by profession; and physicians assure us, that, in his gospel, he has given a more accurate account of the diseases which Jesus cured than any other New Testament writer: that he often uses medical terms in his description of the miracles which were wrought. He was a good and careful thinker, not at all credulous, but disposed to prove all things, holding fast only to the good and true. He wrote his gospel (perhaps you know that he was the author of the book of Acts, also) in Greece, about 35 years after the ascension of Jesus. He was associated with Paul in his travels, went with him to Rome, and continued there during the imprisonment of the apostle. Historians are not agreed in regard to the time or manner of his death. Some affirm that he suffered as a martyr; others, simply, that, in due time, he "fell asleep," or died a natural death. We are sure that his talents, learning, and time were given to the diffusion of the Christian faith. Lastly, and

4th, of JOHN, the beloved disciple, so termed because of his mild and gentle spirit, and because he most resembled his and our Master. He was born in Judea, near the sea, or lake, of Galilee. Zebedee, his father, was a fisherman; and John, probably, engaged in his father's business until he became a preacher of glad tidings. You must not, from this fact, conclude that they were certainly poor men, for then, at least, men of wealth were engaged in the business, and I suppose many now are. John was the youngest apostle, and "the disciple whom Jesus loved;" you may recollect that he leaned on the bosom of Christ at the "Last Supper." He, only, was present, of all the apostles, when Jesus was crucified, - and Jesus commended his mother to this disciple's care. After the resurrection of Jesus, John preached "the gospel" in various parts of Asia.

He wrote his gospel at Ephesus, and, by his labors, the truths of Christianity spread everywhere among men. The story sometimes told, that he was put into a caldron of burning oil, by a Roman emperor, and came out unharmed, is not true. He lived to a very advanced age, and died when not far from 100 years old. Late in life, when too feeble to preach, he was often carried into the meetings of the disciples, at his own request, and, stretching out his hands, as he sat in his chair, was wont to say, "Little children, *love* one another." And, when asked why he so often gave this precept, he would say, "If this be obeyed, it is the Lord's command, and it sufficeth."

Children, will you think of that precept?

Conversing with two lads once, I asked one, Who wrote the Bible, good men, or bad men? "Good men, of course," was the response. "But how do you know they were *good* men?" I rejoined. And he said, "Because," - a very common and very foolish answer, - and was silent. "I think," said the other lad, the younger of the two, "that good men wrote the Bible, because *good* men *love* the Bible, and *wicked* men don't."

Can you give another reason as good?

Now I have told you, briefly, of the four evangelists. They were good men, honest-minded and sincere. Wicked men, all men, act from motives. But *they* could have had no motive to deceive. They lost friends, and wealth, and honor, and ease, and gained contempt, persecution, and suffering, by preaching the gospel. Their conduct is full evidence that they were pure and good men. And, if they were good men, they wrote *the truth*; and, by their labors we have a correct and faithful account of the life of Jesus. Study these books, and by them be made wise. Above all, remember the precept of John, "Little children, love one another."

MAY-DAY.

BY MRS. NANCY T. MUNROE.

It is spring, - a backward spring, it is true, for now it is the first week in May, and not a flower to be seen except the yellow dandelion, not a blossom even on a cherry tree; nothing is green but the grass, and that - yes, that is very green, especially this piece before my window; it seems a relief to look upon it.

Poor May-day revellers! May-day this year was pleasant; that is, the sun shone, the sky was blue, and the grass was green, in spots at least; but the cold north wind was blowing, and one needed to be told it was the first of May.

The sun was higher than usual on such occasions, when the children came upon our hill; - yet they did come with wreaths and May-poles, but, ah! the flowers were artificial. Some of the children had on sun-bonnets and thin shawls; they should have worn hoods and cloaks, and then they might have been comfortable. But it takes a great deal to discourage children from going "Maying."

Our hill is a famous place for children on May-day, for it is green and pleasant; it is glorious to run down its sides, and pleasant to sit on its banks, which once were forts, and behind which, in less peaceful days, lurked soldiers with weapons of war. Ah, those children were a pleasant sight, and as I heard their glad laughter, and saw them chase each other down those green banks, I said, Peace is better than war.

"Please, ma'am, will you tell me what time it is?" said a little girl, coming forward from one group of children.

"Quarter of nine," was the reply.

"I didn't think it was so late; did you?" said she, turning to her companions. They had been out perhaps two hours, and thought it was most noon, and back they went to their sports.

Soon I heard a sound of weeping. I went to the door, where stood a group of children around the pump; one poor shivering child, looking blue and cold, was having her hands and face washed by another, with water cold from the pump, the tears streaming down her cheeks, and she sobbing piteously.

"What is the matter, little girl?"

"Oh," said the one who was performing the washing operation, "she fell from the top of the hill to the bottom, and made her nose bleed and hurt her dreadfully."

The poor child still sobbed and shivered. We carried her in, set her down before a hot coal fire, and tried to warm her red hands. Her little companions came and stood beside her, and told her not to cry; but, oh! she was so cold, and "the tops of her fingers did ache so!"

And this was going a Maying! But yet, next year, these very girls, I doubt not, will start with just as buoyant hearts for May-day sports, forgetful of the fall, the cold, and all inconveniences. Ah, childhood's hopeful heart is a blessed thing!

I well remember now a May-day of by-gone years. Then we had a queen, a tent, and a table set with numberless delicacies. We had rare sport that day. The weather was not as cold as the day of which I have been speaking; we had a few *real* flowers, and some hardy girls even appeared in white dresses. The forenoon passed pleasantly; numerous visitors thronged to see us, and we were the happiest of all May-day revellers. But all pleasure must have an end. Soon word came that we must surrender the sails of our tent, for the owner had need thereof. This caused a general *strike*, and, in the confusion which ensued, a boy had the misfortune to sit or fall upon the queen's straw bonnet, which had been laid aside for her flowery crown. It was literally smashed, unfit for further use. "Ah what will mother say?" was all the disappointed queen could say. Some few laughed at the queer, misshapen thing, but more looked on with sad countenances, for it was the queen's best bonnet.

We separated, tired, and, it may be, a little out of humor; but yet, a few days made everything bright again; we remembered the pleasure with pleasure, and thought of the disappointments only to laugh over them.

And that bent, spoiled bonnet! When the ex-queen appeared in a fine new one, with gay ribbons, many looked on, and almost wished that they had been so fortunate as to have had their bonnets spoiled.

As I look back, other May-days throng upon my mind. The memories of some of these are sad, yea, very sad! One was the birth-day of a little one who now rests beneath the green sod. And well do I remember another bright May morning, when I wandered out over the hill, holding the hand of a little fair-haired child within my own. Her tiny basket was filled with flowers the children had given her, and her bright, sunny face was radiant with smiles. That was her first May-day walk, and much did the little being enjoy it.

It was her last! Ere the spring breezes came again, she lay within her little shroud. The snows of winter fell silently upon her little grave, by the side of him who had gone before, and, ere another May-day, the sod was green above them.

These are the memories that come over me when I look out upon the revellers; yet just as well do I love to see them at their sports, and I can look upon their light, graceful forms, and hear their merry laughter; and, though my heart goes to the grave-yard and mine eyes rest upon the spot, yet I can smile upon the gay, living creatures before me, for I know that childhood is a glad and joyous thing, and that these beings are the light and joy of some homes, and I pray that these homes may be never darkened by Death's shadow crossing the threshold. These my May-day reveries have begun lightly, and ended, as May-days themselves have done, in sad thoughts. But sad thoughts and life's troubles are, or ought to be, the heart's discipline. For this purpose do they come to us, and we should go forth from them purer and better.

THE SNOW-DROP.

BY MRS. M.A. LIVERMORE.

The gentle, laughing, spring had come
With eye and cheek so bright;
The bird glanced through the clear, blue air,
On wing of golden light;
And earth, in gladness, lay and smiled,
To see the beauteous sight.

The streams went singing to the sea,
And dancing to their song;
Its carpet, had the young grass spread
The hills and vales among;
Yet not a flower its bloom had shed,
The fresh green earth along.

Not yet the violet had unsealed
Its blue and loving eye;
Nor had the primrose dared unfold,
For fear that it might die;
And on the tree-tops shook the leaves,
Which oped to kiss the sky.

But so it chanced, one gentle day,
While softly wept the rain,
And sadly sighed the mourning breeze,
The flowers to see again;

A silvery snow-flake fell to earth,
Escaped from winter's chain.

And daintily it laid itself
Where greenest grass was spread,
And where the bland and warm south-wind,
Soft-footed, loved to tread,
And here the white-robed fugitive
Made for itself a bed.

The flower-goddess smiled to see
This new-born snow that fell;
"I'll change it to a flower," said she
"By magic touch, and spell;
For 'twill be long ere blossoms ope,
That spring doth love so well."

Then with a wand of living light,
She touched the feathery snow;
And on it, radiant from her cheek,
There streamed a sunny glow.
Forth from the tiny, crystal flake,
The pearly petals came;
The stem sprang up - there waved a flower, -
The SNOW-DROP was its name!

CAGING BIRDS.

I never liked the idea of rearing birds in cages; of confining those little creatures, that seem to enjoy liberty most of all God's vast family, in the little, stinted prison-house of a cage. Girls seldom incline to keep them caged; I wish, fewer women did; but boys seem almost to possess a different nature. Many really enjoy taking the little helpless fledglings from the nest, hid away so slyly among the thick boughs of the forest-tree; crowding two, three, or even four, into one cage, oftentimes not eighteen inches square. They are even so heartless as to laugh at the fluttering, slapping, and beating of the poor prisoner against the wiry walls of his gloomy, unnatural home.

To be sure, I once owned a caged bird. It was a robin. A dear brother had kept him several years, and, on leaving home for a residence in Boston, where he could not take care of the bird, he gave him to me. It was not at a season of the year when we could safely release him from confinement; and, besides that, our oldest brother had taught him to whistle parts of several tunes, and we feared, moreover, that he might suffer even in the best season of the year, from the fact of his having been taken when so young from other robins. Confinement, probably, does not destroy the instinct of birds, so that they would starve if released. After having been an inmate of our family nine years, having suffered countless frights and manglings from the many kittens we had kept in the time, he at last died by the claws of the family cat, when released one fine afternoon for an airing, and to have his cage cleaned.

I never since have wished to own a caged bird. The song of a canary bird, born and reared in a cage, never pleases me like the cheerful warbling or merry whistle of the wild, free birds of our woodlands. The one seems but the expression of a cheerful forgiveness of unkind treatment, the bursting forth of a happy nature in spite of man's cruelty; while the other seems a free outpouring of perfect happiness, and the choicest notes of a grateful little being directed to the good GOD of nature.

I know we often hear of happy, contented little pet birds; yet I never saw one that did not seem to prefer the freedom of an out-of-door excursion on the strong, free wing, to the hopping, swinging, perching, and fluttering, within a narrow cage. The taming and petting of sparrows, robins, yellow-birds, snow-birds, and swallows, round the doors or windows of one's house, I admire. There is nothing inhuman in this practice. It rather calls forth some of the better feelings of the heart - gives pleasure to us and the birds, yet violates no law of nature.

I here give you a little story of a pet swallow that I met with in a little English book, which, perhaps, few of you have read. The children named in the story were certainly kind-hearted towards their little pet, and very indulgent. Mark well their reward! Some of you may be induced to imitate them; at least, I hope you will not again be so selfish as to cage a bird for his song, while, with the exercise of a little patience and kindly attention, you can tame them so easily at your door.

THE PET SWALLOW.

One day we had been out gathering primroses, and, to put the pretty pale flowers neatly into baskets, we had sat down under one of the windows in the old church tower. Mary was sitting next the wall, when something touched her shoulder, and fell on her knee. It was a young swallow, without any feathers, that had fallen, or perhaps had been thrown, out of the nest, by some quarrelsome brother or sister.

The poor primroses were cast away, and every little hand was ready to seize the prize. When we found it was not killed, or even hurt, by its fall, some called for a cage; others said, "Let us put it back in the nest; we do not know what to give it to eat; we may be sure it will die." And this seemed so very true that we were all obliged to agree; but, alas! the poor swallow having built in a false window of the tower, there was no way of getting to the nest, and so the cage was brought, and the little bird did not die, but grew bigger and prettier every day, until at last it could skim through the room on its pretty, soft wings, and would dive down to us, and light upon our shoulders, or let itself fall into our hands. How we did love that little bird! and oh, how sorry we were one day, when it flew out at the window! We all ran down to the lawn; we were quite sure it would never come back to us again, for it seemed so happy to be free; and we watched it flying here and there - now high in the air, now close down to the ground. We had called our pretty bird Fairy, and it really seemed like a fairy now; one moment it was quite out of sight, the next so near it almost touched us. At last, Fred gave a long, loud whistle; when he began, it was up in the air, high, high above our heads, but, before the sound passed away, it was fluttering its pretty dark wings upon his face. From this time Fairy was allowed to go free; and it would skim about before our windows all day long, coming in from time to time to pay us visits, and to sleep at nights in its old post on the top of one of our little beds in the nursery.

At last August came, and then our pretty Fairy skimmed through the air, far, far beyond the reach of Fred's whistle, for it had set out, with all the other swallows, on its long voyage across the seas.

We had never thought of this, - never thought that our faithful Fairy would so leave us, - and it was many days before the hope of its coming back next year could make us feel at all happy again.

But Fairy, our own dear little Fairy, *did* come back, and it remembered us all, as if it had been away only for a few hours, instead of nearly eight whole months.

It was a very happy day, the day that Fairy came back, and it seemed to feel as much joy as we did; first it flew to Mary, and then to Fred, and then to one after the other, twittering its wings, and rubbing its pretty black head on our hands or faces, as we see dogs and cats do when they want to show great kindness.

It flew to the top of the little bed at night, pecked at the window when it wished to get out in the morning, and would dart down at Fred's whistle as readily as it had been used to do the year before. In short, notwithstanding the long voyage it had made, Fairy seemed to have forgotten neither its old friends nor its old ways.

When it came near the time for the swallows to fly away again, we grew very sad at the idea of losing our pretty Fairy: some thought it would be wise to put it into a cage, and keep it there until all the others were gone; while some, who were wiser, said it was Fairy's nature to go away, and that Fairy must go. But what do you think was our joy to find, that, of its own good will, Fairy stayed with us? All the others went away; and, whether it had grown fonder of us, or that it had not liked the long voyage it had been led into by the example of others, I cannot say; but for four winters it stayed always with us, taking a flight now and then in the open air, but spending the greatest part of the day in the school-room, till summer came, when it would again join its friends, and always build its nest in the very window from which it had fallen into Mary's lap.

Six years had passed since then, but what now became of it we could never learn. For a long time we hoped it had gone again over sea and land, to visit far countries with all the others, but whether it had or not we never knew, for we saw our pretty Fairy no more.

LAST PAGE.

The last bright page before you,
Kind reader and good friend,
Is of another Annual
The very pleasant end.

Our Book's communication
To goodly themes applied,
None of its pages would we wish
To change, expunge, or hide.

With us be Life's brief pages,
When looking back to youth,
So filled with kindly words of love,
And timely Christian truth,

That with an honest confidence
In what our deeds shall say,
With steady and firm hand we write
Our "last page," and away!

www.ingramcontent.com/pod-product-compliance
Lightning Source LLC
Chambersburg PA
CBHW020547310726
48979CB00008B/1127/J

* 9 7 8 1 4 2 1 8 0 0 7 7 6 *